MW00943850

Santa's Kiss

LITTLE CAKES, BOOK NINE

PEPPER NORTH
PAIGE MICHAELS

Copyright © 2022 by Pepper North & Paige Michaels

All characters and events in this book are fictitious. And resemblance to actual persons living or dead is strictly coincidental. The characters are all over the age of 18 and as adults choose to live their lives in an age play environment. All rights reserved.

No part of this book may be reproduced in any form or by any electronic or mechanical means, including information storage and retrieval systems, without written permission from the author, except for the use of brief quotations in a book review.

This is a series of books that can be read in any order. You may, however, choose to read them sequentially to enjoy the characters best. Subsequent books will feature characters that appear in previous novels as well as new faces.

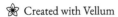 Created with Vellum

About the Book

Welcome to Little Cakes, the bakery that plays Daddy matchmaker! Little Cakes is a sweet and satisfying series, but dare to taste only if you like delicious Daddies, luscious Littles, and guaranteed happily-ever-afters.

Stuffie love is wonderful, but it's no substitute for a Daddy's affection.

After investing in the store franchise of her dreams, Rose Stewart creates cuddly friends for stuffie fans of all ages. A true Little at heart, the only thing missing from her life now is the Daddy of her dreams.

Adam Connell needs a gift for his niece's birthday, and with some holiday magic he finds so much more than just the perfect teddy bear at Stuff-It. The enchanting woman wearing a Santa cap and singing Christmas carols off-tune is the Little he's long been searching for.

Chapter One

Rose was giddy as she skipped around her shop, Stuff-It, double-checking to make sure all the empty stuffie bodies were in their correct bins, the floor was cleared of fluff, and there were plenty of cute outfits arranged on hangers in perfect little rows.

She loved this time of year, and she couldn't keep herself from singing Christmas carols as she spun in circles. Her current earworm was "Toyland." She didn't know all the words, so she just made them up, giggling. She was off-key and probably sounded like a warped vinyl, but she didn't care.

Her last customer had finished filling his new fluffy friend fifteen minutes ago. The mall would be closing soon.

As she belted out yet another line about boys and girls and toys that probably made no sense at all, she spun toward the heavy gate, intent on dragging it across the front of her shop and locking up for the night.

Suddenly, a hand popped out of nowhere and landed on the heavy metal frame just as she was about to pull it free from its pocket in the wall. Rose gasped and nearly jumped out of her skin. The silly lyrics she'd been singing stopped short.

Heart racing, she leaped back, eyes wide as she stared at the large man looming close. Since her shop was located in the mall, she rarely felt threatened or unsafe. After all, even though most of the shops were closing for the night, there were still dozens of people milling around in the wide hallway.

"I'm so sorry, ma'am. I didn't mean to frighten you." The guy took a step back and held up both hands. He was breathing heavily as if he'd run through the mall to get to her.

He didn't look dangerous. He looked...kind, actually. And sincerely sorry. He was big though. Broad and tall. Fit. He was also alone. He didn't have a child with him, or even an adult.

Rose quickly estimated him to be about forty with a thick head of hair that was graying prematurely around the edges. He had a short trimmed beard that was grayer than the rest of his hair.

If she'd seen him anywhere else at any other time, she would have found him drool-worthy. Heck, part of her did now, but the hairs on the back of her neck were still standing up from his shocking arrival.

He swallowed and took another small step back. "I really scared you. I'm terribly sorry," he repeated. "I got stuck in a meeting at work and couldn't get to the mall any sooner. I really, really need a gift for my niece."

The man drew in a deep ragged breath and continued, talking so fast it was hard to keep up. "It's her birthday tomorrow, and she asked me for a Stuff-It. She's only four, so I still dote on her for every birthday and holiday. I've never even heard of Stuff-It until this morning when she told me all about it while I was supposed to be working."

When the man smiled, Rose finally regained some of her composure. He meant her no harm. He just needed a gift.

"Forgive me?" He lifted a brow and held out a hand. "Adam Connell."

Rose glanced down at his large hand and took a deep breath before squaring her shoulders and standing as tall as she could. At five-five, there wasn't a whole lot she could do to seem or feel larger next to Adam Connell. "Rose Stewart." She hoped her voice didn't shake.

"Nice to meet you, Rose. I can see you were about to lock up for the night. I don't suppose I can talk you into staying open for a few more minutes to sell me a stuffed animal?"

She glanced around, noticing there were several shoppers talking near her shop. In addition, there were still about six customers in the lotion and candle store across from hers.

There was no reason to feel threatened. *I'm fine.* She finally smiled. "Of course. I don't like to disappoint four-year-old nieces on their birthdays."

Adam smiled broader. "Thank you so much. I owe you."

As she turned toward the row of empty stuffie bodies, she bit her bottom lip. Adam was delicious. There was no denying the effect he had on her now that she was calm and had found her wits. Tall, dark, and handsome. He looked like the sort of man who would feature as the model on the front of one of her favorite Daddy books.

Stop thinking like that, Rose. Focus. Sell the man a Stuff-It without drooling over him. "Do you know what sort of Stuff-It your niece might like? Bear? Dog? Bunny? Another animal?"

When she tipped her head back to meet Adam's gaze, she found him concentrating as he scanned the row of choices. "Hmm. I'm not sure, but I know the only color she's interested in these days is pink." He pointed at the bin of pink fluff a few feet away. "What's that one?"

Rose snagged it from the bin. "This one is an elephant." She held him up so his front legs were reaching out as if he wanted a hug. "He's been waiting for the perfect child to claim him. Or her."

When Adam didn't say anything for a few seconds, Rose looked up from the elephant to the man and found him staring at her instead of the stuffie. His lips were lifted slightly at the corners, making his eyes crinkle.

Suddenly Rose realized she'd been talking about the

elephant as if she were introducing the fellow to a toddler, not a grown man. She pursed her lips and held her breath.

Adam was still looking at her, still smiling. Indulgently? He lifted a hand and slowly reached out. For a moment, she thought he was going to stroke her cheek, but at the last second, he jerked his attention to the stuffie and patted the elephant awkwardly on the head instead.

Adam's voice was lower and softer when he spoke again. "She's perfect. I'm certain Amelia will say she's a girl. I wouldn't dare name her, but I'd bet my last dollar she'll be named Sally or Betsy. Every time Amelia introduces me to her entourage, those are the two names she seems to have assigned to nearly all of them."

Rose's face heated as she tried to relax. Adam made her feel more self-conscious than any man had in a long time. Wouldn't it be amazing if he were a Daddy? *Her* Daddy?

She stared into space for a moment, picturing this hottie as her Daddy, holding her hand while she skipped along beside him, needing to skip just to keep up with his long strides.

Finally, she shook the absurd visual from her mind when she realized Adam had spoken again. "I'm sorry. My mind wandered. What were you saying?"

He smiled again. "I've decided to make two Stuff-Its tonight. I want the second one to be your choice. Make the perfect stuffie exactly how you would do it if you were the one shopping for a new stuffie tonight."

Rose felt herself grinning as she pulled her shoulders back and glanced at the bins. Every once in a while she got a customer who asked her to make the Stuff-It of her choice. Usually an older person purchasing the Stuff-It as a gift. They didn't care which one it was.

The prospect always made Rose giddy. She loved pretending she was picking one out for herself. It was silly, of course. After all, she owned the shop. She could make any stuffie she wanted with any accessories she wanted any day of the week.

She didn't though because somehow it didn't seem special to own a stuffie she bought herself without the help of a Daddy to guide her. She had stuffed and outfitted about a dozen Stuff-Its to use as displays around the shop, but she didn't have a single one on her shelf at home in her personal collection.

"You sure?" she asked, twisting back to look at Adam. Why would he want to buy a second one?

"Positive. I'll pick out everything for the elephant. You make a second one exactly how you'd like it."

"Okay..." She had to force herself not to clap her hands together. She wasn't in Little space here. This was her business. She was always professional while at work. Still... It was impossible not to get a bit excited, especially since no one but Adam was around to see her, and he certainly didn't seem to judge her enthusiasm.

It took her several seconds to decide which stuffie most appealed to her this week. It was always changing. Finally, she opted for one of the newer stuffies—a beagle with long floppy ears.

She felt lighter on her feet as she snatched him up and had to remind herself not to hug him to her chest. *Shop owner, Rose. Not a Little. You're at work.*

To be honest, she was always at work these days. She was trying to run a successful business after all. She hadn't had time to satisfy her Little side much in months.

If she wasn't mistaken, Adam's eyes were dancing with indulgence as she turned toward the machine they would use to fill the beagle and elephant with fluff. Luckily, she hadn't turned it off yet for the night.

She held the beagle out toward Adam. "Would you mind holding him while I fill the elephant?"

"Of course." Adam carefully arranged the beagle in his huge

hands so that his head was upright. He also petted the little guy's ears so they would lie flat.

A small gasp escaped Rose's lips before she jerked her gaze to Adam's. Was he making fun of her? He didn't look like it. He still looked like the most perfect, kind, amazing Daddy she'd ever seen. Was it possible he was a Daddy? Just because he was in her shop buying a Stuff-It or two didn't make him a Daddy. It just made him an amazing uncle.

Adam surprised her further when he lifted the beagle to his ear first and furrowed his brows as if he were listening to something the dog was telling him. When he lowered the stuffie, he glanced at its face and nodded. "I think that's a great idea. How about if I hold you up so you can watch Sally or Betsy get stuffed. That way you'll know what to expect and won't be scared when it's your turn."

Rose giggled. It was impossible not to. She hoped to God Adam wasn't making fun of her. She'd be mortified if that were the case. "I think he's seen dozens of stuffies get their fluff today from the bin. If he's telling you he's scared, he's pulling your leg."

Adam glanced at the beagle and lifted the dog's mouth to his ear again. "What's that?" He paused for a moment as though listening to a response, nodding a few times. Finally, he lowered the dog and returned his attention to Rose. "He says he was situated facing the boring wall all day and missed out on the action. He's been praying someone would at least lift him up to move him around a bit for hours so he could see what all the excitement was about."

Rose was pretty sure her smile split her face in half. She was trembling. Adam was too good to be true. She jerked her gaze back to the beagle. She needed to focus. "I'm terribly sorry you were facing the wall. My apologies. I'll pay more attention in the future to ensure all your friends are facing the room when I open each morning."

Adam glanced at the bins. "Maybe I could help you get

them arranged better after we finish these so you won't be rushed in the morning tomorrow."

Rose blinked at him. Was he serious? "You don't have to do that."

"It would be my pleasure. I hate disappointed stuffies." He winked at her.

She stared at him for a few seconds before holding the elephant's opening up to the fluff machine. While she concentrated on filling the stuffie, she tried hard not to think about Adam and the way he'd inched closer.

The way he was holding the beagle at just the right angle so the dog could watch. The way he smelled—a masculine scent that made her panties wet and her breasts feel heavy. The way he accidentally, or perhaps intentionally, brushed against her as her elbow stuck out and skimmed along his muscular forearm.

Okay, that last one might have been all her. She wasn't sorry. She loved how his shirtsleeves were carefully rolled up almost to his elbows. Not haphazardly but precisely. He was also wearing fine gray dress pants and a tie, but he'd loosened the tie at some point during the day and unbuttoned the top button of his pale blue shirt.

As she finished filling the stuffie, she noticed his shoes were excellent quality and perfectly buffed. She wondered what he did for a living, but she wasn't about to ask. That would be too personal, nosy. He was a customer.

Somehow she was going to have to finish this transaction and watch him walk away. Chances were she would never see him again. How many Stuff-Its could one man buy his niece?

She was certainly going to enjoy every moment she had with him though. She would always remember this odd interaction. It would undoubtedly feature in her dreams for weeks if not years. That's how potent and magnetic Adam was.

Even if he were the most perfectest Daddy on the planet, she didn't have time at this stage in her life to devote to *any* relationship, let alone an age-play dynamic. She was focused on her business. Nothing else. It was doing well, but it needed coddling and attention for a few more years before she could relax.

The marketing alone was a time suck. The only way to stay present in people's minds was to run ads and keep up with her social media platforms. That side of the business wasn't her favorite, but it had to be done.

With an internal sigh, Rose smiled broadly and handed the elephant to Adam, taking the beagle in exchange.

Chapter Two

Adam didn't think he'd stopped grinning from the moment he stepped into this amazing Little girl's space. He still felt bad for scaring the dickens out of her when he'd first approached, but he hoped she'd let him make it up to her. Preferably over dinner. Or maybe a trip to the park. Coffee and swings.

The vision kept morphing until he settled on picturing coffee for him, hot chocolate for her. They would sit on a bench and drink their beverages before he would toss their cups into the trashcan and guide her toward the swings.

The sun would be shining but it would be chilly outside. The swings he was visualizing were in the grassy area across from Little Cakes. As he watched Rose fill the beagle, he wondered if she'd ever been to Little Cakes and what flavor cupcake she preferred.

He'd been there dozens of times with his niece. He liked to spoil Amelia. It drove his sister crazy every time he took her there because she said Amelia spent the rest of the afternoon bouncing off the walls. Adam simply laughed because that's what fun uncles were supposed to do.

Did Rose realize she was whispering to the beagle as she

filled it? Mumbling her apologies and reassuring him he would be so happy once he got his stuffing.

Damn, she was precious. In seconds flat, this Little girl had stolen Adam's heart, turned it upside down, and twisted it into a tight knot. His chest no longer seemed large enough to contain the important muscle.

His offer to arrange all the empty stuffie bodies so they were facing the room had been impulsive and probably absurd, but he'd been trying to come up with any reason in the world to prolong this interaction.

Granted, he was not leaving here without her phone number and a specific date planned, but he already hated the thought of walking away from this adorable shop and not seeing her again for hours. Ten hours would be too many.

And who was he kidding? It wasn't as though he could see her tomorrow morning. He had an early meeting. He doubted Stuff-It opened before ten, but it would be incredibly forward of him to suggest he take her to breakfast anyway.

He had some time to feel her out still. He could probably drag out selecting clothes and other accessories before he spent at least ten minutes making sure all the animals were facing the main section of the room...

Good grief. He'd lost a marble or two. She probably thought he was daft for suggesting such a thing. Besides, he couldn't stall here forever. Eventually the entire mall would be dark.

"There," she declared as she held up the beagle. "Just the right amount of fluff to hold him upright without making him too stiff to snuggle."

Adam reached out to stroke the beagle's hind leg and nodded. "I agree. Just right. What's next? Clothes?"

Her eyes widened. "Goodness, no. First we need to include a heart before we seal up the opening."

Adam palmed his forehead with a bit of dramatic affect. "Of

course. What was I thinking. Do you have those talking hearts that record a message?" He'd seen them on TV, only because Amelia made him watch cartoons sometimes and the commercials during cartoons were geared toward kid-friendly products.

Rose's hair bounced as she spun toward the selection of hearts. She had a cute bob. The front section was pinned up on top of her head with a clip that had a teddy bear on it. A ribbon with the Stuff-It logo hung down a few inches on both sides of the clip. He wondered if she sold those clips. Amelia would love one.

Rose turned around and gave him her wide brown eyes again. She kept switching back and forth between nervous trembling and confident store owner. He was beyond certain she was a Little and suspected she was wobbling between Little space and her adult persona.

He hoped he had something to do with that. Not because he wanted to make her nervous, but he definitely wanted her to default to her Little space when he was nearby.

The stars were aligned tonight. He'd had a crappy day that had lasted far too many hours, and he'd been in a sour mood when he'd arrived. He nearly missed the opportunity to get Amelia a Stuff-It.

His entire demeanor had shifted as he'd jogged toward the shop though. Even from two storefronts away he'd heard the sweet voice of Rose singing. The fact that she couldn't carry a tune just made her even cuter. The fact that she only seemed to know two words to "Toyland" and made the rest up had his heart beating faster than his rushed pace had caused.

As Rose explained the various types of hearts, he watched her. Her full lips were rosy. Her cheeks were pink, and he'd bet they would feel heated to the touch. He caused her to be a little off-kilter. In a good way, he hoped.

Every time she tucked a lock of hair behind one ear or the other, he watched as the thick locks fell right back against her cheek, wishing he had the liberty to stroke her face and tuck the hair back himself.

Patience. He'd already scared the life out of her when he'd instinctively set his hand on the gate, preventing her from pulling it closed.

Call him crazy, but he knew in his soul Rose was the Little girl he'd been looking for his entire adult life. She was filled with happiness and boundless energy. He'd bet she'd been here on her feet working for twelve hours, and still she showed him the same courtesy she undoubtedly showed the first customer of the day.

The thought of her working so many hours made his brow furrow. Little girls shouldn't work so hard. She clearly had an amazing, successful business. He was proud of her in ways he had no right to be yet. But he hoped she had plenty of staff and wasn't the sort of woman who worked thirteen hours a day because she needed her thumb on every aspect.

Adam's mind wandered to the future again. Not the hot chocolate and swings this time but a day in the hopefully-not-too-distant future when she would be in his home. He pictured the room that connected with the master bedroom. He'd already filled it with nursery furniture and toys months ago, hoping it would bring him better luck in finding his Little. Now, he could see Rose sitting in the middle of the room play-ing, concentrating so hard on dressing her stuffies that she didn't know he was standing in the doorway watching her. She was the final component the room needed, and he couldn't wait to see her in it.

What would her hair look like if he put it up in two pigtails? How young did she like to regress when she was in Little space? How much power would she give him to choose her clothes and enforce the kinds of rules Little girls thrived on?

"Adam?"

He jerked his gaze back to hers. "I'm sorry." He pointed

toward the middle bin of hearts. "I'd like the kind I can record something on for my niece."

She smiled, hesitating. "Excellent choice."

It took a few minutes for her to teach him how to record his message, precious minutes he would remember forever as the first time he stood close enough to her to touch her repeatedly. He let his arm brush against hers over and over. He made sure his fingers grazed hers every time she passed him one of the stuffies or hearts.

He took a deep breath and let it out slowly when that part of the process was over, hating how she stepped away to show him the outfits and accessories.

He loved how enthusiastic she was about choosing every detail for the beagle. She kept biting the lower corner of her lip while she stared at the selections, thinking. It was comical since this was her shop and she surely knew every single item on every rack as well as how many more she had in back.

Rose wasn't fully in her adult space though. She'd slipped further into Little space as time passed. By the time she was putting jeans and a T-shirt on the beagle, she was nearly fully Little. She giggled as she tucked his hind legs into the jeggings.

Every inch of her made his heart race. She was perfection.

Suddenly, a thought struck him that made him freeze and panic. *What if she already has a Daddy?* It wasn't unreasonable. Any Daddy would snatch her up as soon as he met her. She was sunshine and warmth. Sweetness and honey.

Rose turned toward Adam with the finished beagle in her hand, lifted him up, and made his head bounce as he clearly spoke. "Ruff!"

Adam chuckled. "I bet he's a lot happier now. It was kind of you to ease his mind while he was scared."

She shrugged. "It's my job. Can't have the stuffies nervous and upset."

"Indeed." He carried the elephant, the dance leotard, the

tutu, and the ballet shoes over to the counter and set them down.

He waited until she processed his credit card and carefully tucked the elephant into the bag. As she lifted the beagle to add it to the carrier, he stopped her, saying, "That one is for you. Ruff told me he needs to belong to you."

"What? You can't do that," she protested, looking completely surprised.

"Why not? Ruff deserves to have the owner he loves. He's bonded to you. Look at those big brown eyes. He already adores you."

Adam watched her gaze at the puppy. He could see her struggle to deny the connection between them but couldn't. With a soft cry of delight, the shop owner pulled the stuffie close and hugged it tightly.

"I don't know what to say," she told him with tears filling her eyes.

"'Thank you' works for now," he answered, feeling himself smile as she held the stuffie to her chest as if she'd never let him go.

"Thank you, Adam."

"You're very welcome. Ruff is very happy to be with you."

"I love him. I don't have any stuffies. I promised myself when I opened the business that I wouldn't take the merchandise home. It's hard to meet my financial goals if I'm the one buying everything."

"Perfect. You kept your promise to yourself, Ruff got a home, and you have a stuffie who needed to be yours. That's a win, win, win in my book," he pointed out. "Now you need to find homes for all the other stuffies."

Adam glanced around the store. "That reminds me, I'll start situating the rest of these stuffies so they can see better."

"You don't have to do that," Rose murmured softly. "I can do it after you leave or in the morning."

When he glanced at her, she was biting that lower lip again.

He hoped to God he was reading her correctly and that she didn't want him to leave any more than he himself wanted. "It's no problem at all. How much more work do you need to do tonight before you can go home?"

Adam busied himself arranging the first layer of stuffies in the first bin while he asked that question, hoping he wasn't spooking her.

"Nothing else. I just need to lock up and..." She lifted her gaze to him and stiffened. "I hope you're not an ax murderer who plans to follow me to my car and kill me."

He stopped moving and turned to fully face her. He hated the renewed fear in her eyes, but he was also glad she had the sense to question her environment and ensure she was safe at all times.

Go big or go home, Adam. He took a deep breath. "I'm not an ax murderer, Rose. I'm a Daddy, and I'm concerned about how you get safely to your car at night."

She swallowed as she absently hugged the beagle against her chest. "Do you mean you're a father and you have children?"

He shook his head. "Nope. I'm not a father. I have no children. I'm a Daddy." He took a tentative step closer to her before reaching out to gently lift her chin. "And you're the cutest Little girl I've ever set eyes on. Please tell me you're single."

She swallowed again. "We just met."

"It feels like I've been here for hours while at the same time it's been moments. Not enough of them."

When she bit her lip again, he used his thumb to pluck the swollen flesh free, loving the sweet gasp that escaped her lips. She oh-so-subtly tipped her cheek into his palm. "I think so too," she whispered.

Adam gave a silent, internal fist pump. *Thank. You. God.* "You didn't answer my question. Do you have a Daddy, Rose?" He needed to know this detail before he took things even one more step further.

"No," she answered.

17

He exhaled all the oxygen from his lungs. "Thank goodness. I hate that I have a busy schedule this week, but I hope you'll agree to go out with me as soon as we're both available at the same time."

She blinked those big brown eyes at him, her cheeks adorably flushed. "I think I'd like that."

He couldn't stop the relieved smile. "Good." Suddenly, he had a new idea that replaced the hot chocolate vision. "Have you ever been to Little Cakes in the strip mall?"

She nodded. "Lots of times. It's the best."

"How about if we meet there for our first date. It will be open and public. Little girls should never give a stranger their address until they're certain he means them no harm."

She smiled broadly. "I'm glad you said that. I was afraid you would want to pick me up at my home... Well, my apartment. That's my home now."

He shook his head. "Not for the first date. However, if you've spent much time at Little Cakes, I bet we have some mutual friends who can vouch for me. Do you know Tarson, the baker?"

She nodded. "Yes. I know most of the employees. They're, uh..."

Adam grinned. "Little. I know. I've seen several of them at Blaze from time to time. I've never seen you there."

"I just moved here to open this shop about six months ago. I don't have close friends yet. Except for trips to Little Cakes, I've been working long hours for months."

He frowned, not wanting to overstep yet but feeling worried about her at the same time. "Little girls shouldn't work so hard."

She shrugged and took a step back, freeing herself from his touch. "I might be Little on the inside, but I haven't had much time to practice lately. I don't have a Daddy and I'm nearly always in my adult headspace, working long hours. Opening a business is time consuming. I don't have a choice yet, but I do have several employees who are nearly ready to be left here alone for several hours. I was hoping to start doling out more responsibilities soon."

"You should do that. If you don't, you'll wear yourself out. Besides, I'd like to spend as much time as I can with you so I can get to know you and vice versa. I'll start to get jealous of the bears and bunnies and puppies if you talk to them more than you talk to me," he teased, glancing at the bins of stuffies.

She giggled, a sound he loved. "You can't get jealous of inanimate objects."

He reached out to clasp his hands over the ears of the beagle she still held. "Shh... Don't talk like that in front of this puppy. He's had a rough day. You're going to hurt his feelings if you insinuate he has none."

She giggled again before turning to set him on the counter with the elephant nestled in the sack.

When she turned back around, he continued the banter. "I know for a fact stuffies have feelings because Amelia tells me so often. Besides, Daddies can get jealous of just about anything that keeps their Little girls away. I bet the owner of Little Cakes has to contend with a Daddy who gets jealous of cupcakes."

The smile that widened on Rose's face made Adam so damn happy. "I suspect you're right. I've met Ellie several times. I've seen her Daddy pop in too. Garrett probably doesn't like sharing her with frosting and sprinkles."

"See? It's not just stuffies. Now, let's get the rest of these friends turned the correct direction so you can get home and get some rest. What time do you usually get to work in the morning?"

She started turning the heads of a bin of unicorns as she spoke. "About nine forty-five. The mall opens at ten."

"Are you a morning person or a night owl?"

"Morning," she answered without hesitation.

"Good. Tomorrow I have an early meeting and I need to go

to my niece's birthday party right after work, but sometimes we can have breakfast dates."

She smiled. "That sounds like fun. Can we get pancakes?"

Yes. She was definitely the most perfect Little girl he'd ever met. A sense of peace washed over him as he watched her face light up. "We can absolutely get pancakes. With lots of syrup." He was glad they were lining up future possibilities. "Can you take a late lunch the day after tomorrow? Can your employees handle the shop for a few hours so we can get cupcakes?"

She seemed to think for a moment and then nodded.

He reached out and cupped her face again. "I'm so glad I caught you just in time tonight. If I'd been a few minutes later, I wouldn't have met the sweetest Little girl I've ever seen."

"I'm glad too." She was smiling, but her cheeks were still flushed and she looked slightly nervous. She should. After all, he was mostly a stranger. A trip to Little Cakes would help ease her mind though. Tarson would vouch for him.

Adam could hardly stand the idea of waiting nearly two full days before he saw her again, but he needed to be patient. If he rushed her, he would scare her.

Chapter Three

Two days later, Rose opened Stuff-It at exactly ten o'clock according to the mall's regulations. The early morning mall walkers were finishing up their laps around the building as customers streamed in to do their Christmas shopping. Rose had stayed late last night to dress the stuffies in the window displays in holiday clothing and add festive ornaments and greenery to the store. She yawned as she pushed the gate open completely.

"You need more sleep, boss," a cheerful voice commented as she walked into the store. The curvy brunette stopped just outside the entrance and smiled. "You decorated. You should have let me know. I love to throw tinsel around."

"Hi, Larisa," Rose greeted her employee. "Does the store look okay?"

"I love it. You'd suggested that we talk about doing more with the store's social media. I'm super stoked to take some pictures of the decorated displays and invite customers to come create special friends for the holiday," Larisa suggested.

"That would be awesome. I'd love to make you Stuff-It's social media guru. Would you be open to trying it for the next month, featuring the Christmas season? If you can create a positive buzz, I'll assign you the job and give you a raise. Until we see if the extra advertising on the different platforms is effective, I can't promise you much, but I'll give you a bonus each week."

"Let's try it. I'm going to be learning in the beginning, so a bonus is great. When customers are raving about the store and piled three deep to the character bins, trying to choose their new best friend, a raise will be even better," Larisa said with a grin.

"I'd happy dance to see that. Just don't make it happen this afternoon. I promised a friend I'd meet them at Little Cakes to chat. Think you'll be okay for a couple of hours by yourself?" Rose asked, watching Larisa's face carefully.

"Of course. I think Amber comes in to help at two before the afternoon rush. We'll be fine," Larisa assured her. "Is it okay if I wear this?"

Rose looked at the funky Santa hat and laughed. "Where did you get that?"

"Three shops down at the bookstore. They have a whole display. Want one?" Larisa asked.

"I think we need several. Go ahead and put yours on and I'll run down when I have a few minutes and buy a few more so we can all wear one. Santa caps all around," Rose cheered.

"I knew I was going to love working here," Larisa said.

"You all are having so much fun!" a customer observed. "I fell in love with the dragon in the window wearing the elf costume. Could I make one for my son?"

"That is the cutest, isn't it?" Larisa agreed with a smile. "Have you been to Stuff-It before?"

"Never. I've seen the store, of course, and heard people talking about making a stuffed animal," the friendly customer commented.

"Let me walk you through the process. Let's find the perfect dragon first. All the stuffable friends are over here. We actually have three colors of dragons..."

Rose watched Larisa guide the shopper to the display. She

and Larisa had clicked immediately during the interview process. Rose had learned to listen to her gut when hiring employees. With only four employees and herself, Rose needed to have people to rely on.

"Miss?" An older man interrupted her thoughts.

"Yes? Can I help you find a new friend?" Rose asked with a smile, sure that this was a grandpa shopping.

"Tomorrow is my anniversary. My wife has quite a collection of stuffies but nothing from your new store. I'd like to make her one, please."

"Of course. We do have gift certificates if you'd like to bring her in to do it herself. That's a lot of fun."

"Oh, I'm afraid she doesn't get out much anymore. Crowds jostle her too much without meaning to cause her pain. Darn arthritis," he shared.

"I'm sorry. It will be just as special if you create a surprise for her. Does she have a favorite animal?" Rose asked, trying not to tear up at the sad story. She couldn't ask but his use of the word stuffie made her think maybe his wife was Little.

"A cat. Black, if you have one."

"I do. Come see if this one is the best choice for her."

As soon as Rose helped him begin the process of choosing all the special features for his stuffie, another customer arrived. The entire morning rushed by with a steady stream of eager stuffed-animal creators. The flow of shoppers fit perfectly with the process of choosing all the fun components and adding the stuffing. Larisa and Rose were busy but not so swamped that they couldn't interact with each person to help them make the best choices.

"I love this cat," Rose confided as she rang up the black cat who now wore a polka-dot nightshirt. He'd added his voice saying "I love you" and a lavender scent to help his wife sleep.

"Bethie will adore it," he answered confidently. "I think I saw some polka-dot nightgowns in the store across the way. I'm off there next."

"That's perfect!" Rose smiled as she watched the older man walk out of the store carrying the stuffie as if it were the most precious gift on earth. Bouncing on her toes with happiness that a stuffed animal from her shop would be so cherished, Rose turned to help the next customer.

After Larisa returned from her lunch break, Rose dashed down the hallway to the bookstore. To her delight, they also had smaller Santa's hats that would fit perfectly on the stuffies' heads. A cute idea of highlighting a different stuffed animal each day by placing the hat on its head popped into her mind. There was only one Santa anyway. Not all the stuffies could wear a hat on the same day.

Catching sight of the time, she rushed back to the store. It was almost time for her date with Adam. She'd hoped to get a message from him today, but her phone had remained stubbornly blank. They'd texted a bit yesterday. Adam had even sent her a picture of his favorite niece and her new elephant friend, Pinkie. It seemed that his niece had expanded her choice of names for her new friend, abandoning the usual Sally and Betsy for something much more appropriate for the rosy pachyderm.

Now, it seemed strange that she hadn't heard from him. Maybe she should try to call in case he'd changed his mind. As she walked into the store, Larisa pantomimed holding a phone to her ear as she waited for a child to make their choice of a cream or dark brown teddy bear.

Dashing to the cash register where she'd left her phone, Rose checked the screen. One missed call and a message. She'd missed him. With a heavy sigh, Rose played the message, fearing the worst.

Hi, Rose! I know you're busy, but I wanted to confirm our date at Little Cakes at two? Are you still able to make it?

Immediately, Rose pressed the call button to connect with

him. Just hearing his deep voice made her smile. "Hi, Adam. I'm sorry I missed your call."

"No problem. Are we still on for a cupcake lunch?" he asked. "If you have time, we could meet at Nibbles & Bites first for a salad so we can pretend to balance out the calories between healthy and yummy foods."

She hesitated before answering honestly, "I'm afraid I can't take that much time off today."

"I shouldn't either but it is tempting to run away where they can't find me."

Rose heard a bellow in the background for *Boss!* "Sounds like something urgent. Go. I'll see you at two for a cupcake."

"I can't wait, Little girl."

Her phone went black. It was weird for her to miss him after knowing Adam for such a short time, but she did.

Taking a quick sip of the bottle of water she'd grabbed on her way out of Stuff-It, Rose tried to tell herself everything was going to be okay. She gathered her courage and exited the car as she gave herself a continual pep talk on the way to the entrance. Standing outside Little Cakes, she paused to take a deep breath and opened the door. As she walked into the bakery, Rose glanced around, trying to spot Adam. She crossed her fingers, hoping to find him inside.

"Little girl," a familiar voice greeted her, and without think-ing, she rushed forward to wrap her arms around his waist. Immediately, he returned the embrace. "Now that's the kind of welcome a Daddy could grow to love."

"Rose! I wondered who Adam was waiting for!" Ellie called across the shop.

Adam gave her one last squeeze before stepping back to take her hand. "I can't believe we're both regulars here and we've never run into each other. Let's go order and then we can talk."

Nodding, Rose let Adam guide her over to the display counter. "Hi, Ellie. I'm glad to see you."

"How's the Stuff-It store going? I'd love to organize a time for a group of..." Ellie leaned forward to whisper, "Littles to come in and make a stuffie. Do you host private events?"

"I haven't ever done that, but we could definitely set up a time like on a Sunday morning before the mall opens?" Rose suggested.

"Do you have a card? I'll call you when you're not... busy," Ellie said with waggling eyebrows.

Producing her business card from her purse, Rose tried not to react to the friendly baker's words. She glanced at Adam and loved the way his eyes sparkled with amusement. He wasn't at all embarrassed by Ellie's cheerful insinuations.

"Adam and I are here to have a cupcake together. Do you have any suggestions for us?"

"Of course! Our featured cupcake is Santa's Kiss. If you love chocolate, that's the one for you. There's a special treat under the Santa's cap," Ellie shared.

"Like a chocolate candy?" Rose asked.

"That would be what everyone would expect. Tarson and I created our own yummy treat for Santa's cap to hide."

Adam chuckled. "Your smile alone makes me want to find out what that is. I'll take one. What do you think, Rose? Want to try something new?" he asked, squeezing her hand.

"Yes. I'd like to try it as well," Rose answered, staring into his hazel eyes. She'd struggled yesterday to remember what color they were. Filling in that small bit of information helped Rose believe she hadn't made him up. Well, that and having Ellie's approval too!

"Is Tarson around?" Adam asked after paying for the cupcakes and two large glasses of milk.

"He's in back mixing up some batter. I can get him for you," Ellie responded.

"I'd hoped he'd vouch for me so Rose didn't have to worry

that I was a bad character," Adam shared. His easygoing smile softened the harsh reality of his statement.

Tarson suddenly pushed through the door that led to the back room. "Vouch for you? Heck, I've invited you home for dinner with Daisy and me. I'd never let you close to my Little girl if you didn't have my complete confidence," he announced, coming up to thump Adam on the back. "You're dating Rose?"

"I'm hoping to convince her to take a chance on me," Adam responded, looking at Rose.

Ellie beamed. "Is this your first date? Here at Little Cakes? I'm so honored you chose my bakery. Go select your official table. Twenty years from now, you can come back to celebrate the anniversary of your first date. I'll bring everything to you in a flash," she instructed.

As Adam guided Rose to a secluded table by the window, Rose blurted, "Ellie is a sweetheart but she's enthusiastic. I'm sorry."

"I'm not. I think coming back here in twenty years is an incredible idea. I plan to add this to my calendar."

"Really? You think we'll be together in twenty years?" she asked before she could stop herself.

"That's how I feel inside. No pressure on this first date. It's going well, though. Tarson's vouched for me. I've passed the Ellie test. Now all I have to do is convince you to keep me."

"That's sweet of you to say but we both know you could have anyone you wanted," she observed, trying to keep her perspective and not tumble head over heels in love with Adam.

"You're giving me more credit than you should. I'll confess that I have a terrible habit of blowing bubbles and popping them. You may find me totally annoying."

"Like with bubble gum?" she asked curiously.

Suddenly, Ellie appeared, giggling next to them. "Now that's a flavor we haven't considered yet. Bubble gum would be a great cupcake. Thanks, Rose," Ellie said as she placed a fancy tray on the table. With a wave, she disappeared to greet customers as they approached the counter.

Rose leaned forward to unload the beautifully decorated tray, but Adam stopped her by running his hand over her forearm. Confused by his action, she glanced up at him.

"Daddy's job," Adam explained as he placed a glass of milk and a cupcake in front of her with a small stack of napkins and a fork. "There you go. Dig in."

She waited until he had served himself before saying, "Do Daddies take care of everything?"

"I think most Daddies enjoy taking care of their Littles in big and small ways. I know I do."

Nodding, she tried to digest his words and look for any possible hidden meaning. To give herself some time to think, she carefully peeled off the paper wrapper. A funny thought went through her mind. Would he eat the cupcake with a fork or just take a bite? She peeked up at him, trying to guess.

He held the cupcake in his hand. With the wrapper partially removed from one half of the treat, Adam lifted the decorated top to his nose and sniffed the Santa hat. "I think it's something mint flavored. Do you want to try it first or do you want me to make sure it's okay?"

"You."

She watched Adam tilt the cupcake and bite the holiday hat away. Staring at him in surprise, she blurted, "You ate the decoration first."

"Is that against the rules?"

"I've never seen someone eat a cupcake from the top down," she answered in amazement.

"Wait until my next bite," he suggested and held the cupcake back to his lips as if he would bite off the rest of the frosting next. At the last moment, he tilted the cupcake and took a bite from the side, devouring a combination of cake and frosting. A scant bit of frosting clung to his full mustache.

"Anything in my beard?" he asked, brushing his napkin over his full lips.

She'd never been jealous of a napkin before. "Got it. I bet cupcakes and mustaches don't go well together."

"I'll never turn down a cupcake in fear of decorating myself. That's what napkins are for, right? Try yours."

Rose bit into the cupcake and got only a small taste of the center decoration. Looking at the bite mark, she nodded and turned it to face him. "You're right. It is something minty." She scooped some of the frosting onto her finger and tasted the sweetness. "Oh, yum! This is amazing."

"Told you," he answered as he leaned forward to brush frosting from her cheek.

His warm fingers against her flesh felt comforting and personal. Without thinking, she turned her head to press her cheek into his palm. His expression switched from fun-loving to caring in a flash. Rose closed her eyes for a fraction of a second to engrave this cherished feeling into her brain.

"Little girl, you delight me."

"Better than cupcakes?"

"Yes."

Time seemed to freeze as they stared into each other's eyes. The jingle of the door opening reminded them they weren't alone. Regretfully, Rose pulled his hand away from her cheek. Searching for something to break the spell, Rose remembered Ellie's new thought for a featured treat.

"You do something with bubble gum?"

Thankfully, Adam allowed her to change their focus. "I do. I own a bubble gum factory. It's been in the family for years. I'm the next Connell to run it."

"I hadn't put your name together with the company. That must be a fun job."

"Definitely not as fun as your shop. There are days when every machine decides to act up."

"Oh! So you work in the factory. I figured you had managers to do that."

"That's not the Connell style. I've manned every position at the factory. My dad and grandpa thought all the kids needed to work to appreciate their employees. I thank them almost every day."

"Not every day?" she teased.

"Nope. Some days, I wish I had a fancy office with a view."

"So do you still even like bubble gum?"

"Of course. I perform quality control and sample all the flavors. I might just hold the company record for the biggest bubble."

When she looked suitably impressed, he asked, "Do *you* like bubble gum?"

"I do. I haven't chewed it in a while," she admitted, taking another bite of her cupcake. "This is so good."

"I think I might have a favorite flavor now."

"We'll have to come back this month for you to have another one. The special features don't stay around for long." She stopped herself abruptly. *I just asked him out again!*

"I'll look forward to enjoying more frosting with you," he answered gently. "What shall we do for our next date? The zoo? A picnic? Breakfast?"

"I'm so sorry. I'm not a good person to date. I practically live at the store now. I can only sneak away for a short time." Rose paused and looked at her watch before continuing. "Especially now with the holiday season, I need to pull in as many customers as possible and make their experience so memorable that they come back for more."

"Then I'll come to you. What are you doing when the store closes tonight?"

"I have to do some inventory and restock if we're busy up to closing time. I may not have time to do that while Stuff-It is open."

"I'm a good worker. I'll zip in at closing time and help you with whatever you need. After that, we'll see how tired you are."

"I'm usually exhausted," she confessed.

"Then it will be bedtime for you, Little girl."

"Are you sure you're my Daddy?"

"There's no doubt in my mind."

Chapter Four

Looking at the clock for what had to be the four hundredth time, Rose scolded herself, "You're not making the numbers move any faster." Forcing her mind back to the task at hand, she helped newly arriving customers as Amber manned the cash register. The high schooler was a model employee and obviously a good student. She loved wearing the Santa hat and was so cheerful her happiness rubbed off on everyone.

Several teachers had come in to make stuffed friends. All had been delighted to see her. Rose hadn't anticipated her employee drumming up business at school, but it appeared that Amber had shared her amazing job with everyone she knew.

When a large man walked through the door, Rose felt her shoulders settle into place. She hadn't realized how tense she'd become waiting for Adam to show up after their incredible date. Talking to him felt like she'd known him for a long time. It was comfortable but nerve-racking.

"Hi, Adam!" She waved a greeting.

"Hi, Rose."

When she turned back to the counter, Amber squeezed in next to her to whisper, "You know him?"

"I do."

"He's gorgeous. A real silver fox like they talk about in my mom's romance novels," Amber gushed.

"A bit too old for you?" Rose teased.

Sighing loudly, Amber agreed, "Probably. But I can dream."

Rose couldn't stop the giggle that welled from her lips. "You'll have to tell your mom you met a character from her books."

"Oh, I read them, too. They're yummy," the teenager said before adding, "Is it okay if I head home? I have a math test tomorrow."

"Of course. I'm almost ready to close the shop. Go study," Rose urged.

"Thanks, boss!"

Rose watched the bubbly young woman gather her things from behind the counter and head into the mall toward the parking lot with a wave. How long had it been since she'd read a juicy book? Rose resolved that she'd squeeze in a chapter or two soon.

"She seems personable," Adam commented.

"Amber is a great employee. I tried to choose people who fit the fun environment of the shop but who seemed reliable and honest."

"Put me to work. What can I do?" Adam asked.

"You could help me straighten."

"You've got it."

He followed her over to the bin and worked next to her, making sure all the stuffie bodies were ready for eager customers to choose them. His gentle presence as they worked side by side felt wonderful. Adam chatted about the news in the world and told her funny things that had happened at work.

"What's the hardest color to make a gumball?" she asked.

"We tried tie-dye once. It was a royal flop. All the colors just blended together. Who wants gray bubble gum?"

"Yuck. That doesn't sound appetizing."

Rose heard another door in the mall closing and checked the time. "Be right back. I'll close up."

She slid the metal gate across the opening of the shop and turned to pull the glass doors closed.

"Wait! I need to make a..."

Rose studied the man on the other side of the barrier as he spoke. When he fumbled to name some item he needed to buy in the store, she quickly decided not to reopen the door.

"I'm sorry, sir. The mall is closed. Come back tomorrow. Our business hours are from ten to nine," Rose said politely.

The man looked like he would argue as Rose felt Adam approach to stand behind her. He didn't interfere but stood silently.

"I guess I'll make another trip back tomorrow," the man grumbled and he turned and disappeared among the shoppers heading for their cars.

"That was weird," Adam observed.

"It really was. We get all kinds of people here. That makes my job interesting."

"I guess I was lucky you held the store open for me two nights ago, but it probably hadn't been a safe choice for you. I could have been dangerous." He frowned as he faced her.

Rose shrugged. "You didn't put off a creepy vibe like that man. After my initial shock, I felt safe with you."

"Still. It worries me that you might face a predator here at night. Do you walk out alone?" Adam asked.

"Yes. I'm always a bit scared. I've got the cash from the day for the bank deposit," she admitted.

"I don't like that, Little girl."

"One of the responsibilities of the job. I could have a security guard walk me out, but Johnny isn't always available, and his presence seems to draw more attention to me anyway."

"I think you're going to get tired of me, Little girl. Plan for me to be here to walk you to your car each night. Did you get any dinner tonight?"

"No, I'm running on cupcake fumes."

"That's not acceptable. You need to take better care of yourself," Adam commented. "Will you come with me for a late-night snack?"

"I'd like to, but I need to stop at the bank and head home. I didn't sleep too well last night. I was sure I'd ruin our cupcake date," she admitted.

"I enjoyed our time together. I don't live far away. How about if we go to my house after you close up tomorrow for a bedtime snack?"

"Like I'm going to sleep there?" she asked.

"You could. But I think you'd like to move slower to make sure I'm your Daddy. I'm not rushing you, pet. You are worth waiting for. I just want to feed you."

He approached slowly, giving her plenty of time to stop him. Without saying any flowery words, Adam wrapped his arms around her waist and pulled her close. He cupped her cheek just as he had at Little Cakes. His thumb rubbed softly against her skin. Rose felt so cherished.

Rising to her toes, she pressed her mouth against his. Immediately, his hand wrapped around the back of her head and pulled her closer. Adam deepened the kiss, dipping inside to taste her sweetness. His soft moan of desire made her press her body closer to his chest as sweet heat developed inside her. She loved the feel of his hard chest against her. Adam held her as if he never wanted to let her go.

When he finally lifted his head, Rose could only stare at him. Her mom had always told her that she knew Rose's father was the one for her when he kissed her in the hallway at school. Adam's kiss made the men she'd dated before look like rank amateurs. The thought flashed in her mind that she couldn't wait to make love to him. She felt her cheeks heat in response to that racy thought.

"I'd pay money to know what's going on in your mind," Adam whispered.

A clanking noise made them both jerk their attention toward the mall. Johnny, the security guard, stood with a large flashlight in his hand. He yelled loudly to be heard through the glass. "You okay, Rose?"

"I'm good, Johnny. Thank you for checking on me," Rose hollered back and then looked apologetically at Adam.

"I'm glad he's vigilant. He's a nice friend to have." When she nodded, he pivoted to look into the store with his arm still around her waist, holding her close. "What else do we need to do?"

"I think I'm ready to go after I empty the cash register." Rose stepped away to grab the money pouch from her office and her large purse.

Adam automatically moved to block the view from the mall into the store as she removed the cash and coins from the tray. She loved that he thought of so many ways to take care of her. Peeking up at him as she put the last handful of bills into the bank deposit pouch, she found him watching her closely.

"Did those kisses seem different to you?" she asked. When he raised one eyebrow in amusement, she realized how he could take her question wrong. "I mean, were they special?"

"Yes, Rose. They were much more precious. I'm glad you felt that way, too, because I plan to kiss you often."

Nodding, she answered honestly, "I'd like that."

They gathered everything and went out the back entrance. Rose double-checked every step in her closing process. Having Adam there was a distraction.

The employee entrance was empty, and she was pleased to have him with her as she walked through the eerily quiet hallway and into the parking lot. There were a few groups of teenagers standing around the parking lot. Rose was used to their presence. She remembered being young and having nowhere to go to hang out with friends.

"Night, Stuff-It lady!" one called and waved.

"Night!" she answered.

"Everyone knows the stuffie lady," Adam commented.

"I love that my store is gaining a name. It's really more than I ever dreamed."

"Speaking of dreams... You need to go home and get in bed. Want me to follow you home?"

"No, Adam. I'll be fine. Will I see you tomorrow?"

"Yes. I'll have something quick to cook for a late snack just in case you decide to come visit."

Rose gathered her courage and nodded. "I'd like that. We need some time alone to figure out if this is what we think it is."

Adam nodded and stepped forward to kiss her again. The magic that flowed from his kisses made Rose forget where they were. Wolf whistles and cheers drifted across the parking lot in response to the leashed passion they could sense.

Lifting his head, Adam said gruffly, "Go home, pet. Sleep well."

"Let me drive you to your car," she suggested.

"It's right there." He motioned to a large SUV a few rows away.

He helped her into her car. "Put your seatbelt on. Be careful at the bank."

"I will. See you tomorrow."

She watched him disappear as she drove from the parking lot. Rifling in her large purse, she pulled out the adorable friend she'd hidden inside. The beagle looked back at her with wide eyes.

"I know, Ruff! He kissed me. It was so incredible. I'm going to his house tomorrow night. You'll come with me, of course."

Ruff stared back at her with those big eyes.

"I'm going to kiss him again, Ruff. Maybe more. I really think he's the one."

Chapter Five

"Let me put my address in your phone, Rosebud." Adam smiled down at his Little girl as he slid one hand down her back and reached to take her cell from her with the other. They were next to her car, and he glanced around every few seconds to ensure they were safe.

He knew he was being a bit high-handed, but he wanted her to feel comfortable deferring to him when they were together.

His heart warmed when she simply smiled up at him and handed him her phone. "Is this one of those bossy Daddy things?"

"Yep." She understood, and that made him even happier. "Daddies like to take care of their Little girls. You can follow me home in your car, but I'll feel better knowing you have my address in your GPS just in case we get separated at a stoplight or something."

He'd shown up a few minutes before closing time again tonight after spending most of the day thinking about nothing except seeing Rose again. He'd sat through two meetings about a mechanical problem in the plant during the day, struggling to pay close attention the entire time.

Finally, she was going to his house. It would be their first time alone together. He wasn't the typical bachelor with a messy apartment that needed a woman's touch. He was fairly organized and thought his home was warm and inviting. Granted, it didn't hurt that his sister had helped him decorate when he'd moved in.

After entering his address under his contact information in her phone, he handed her the cell and opened her car door to help her inside. "Drive safe, Rosebud."

She giggled. "Is that my new nickname?"

He smiled. "I think so. Do you like it?"

She worried her bottom lip with her teeth before she nodded. "I do. Roses are pretty and the petals are delicate."

"Perfect then because I think you're definitely pretty and delicate."

She giggled again. He loved that sound. "I'm hardly delicate."

"You are to me. Precious." As she got settled in her seat, he grabbed the seatbelt and reached across her to fasten it before stealing a quick kiss.

"Mmm. I like your kisses," she whispered as he eased his head out of her car.

"Good. I'm hoping to kiss you a few more times before the night is over."

"Are you going to make love to me too?" she asked, eyes wide. She immediately clamped her lips together as her cheeks turned red. A second later, she glanced away.

He reached for a thick lock of her hair and stroked it next to her ear. "Eventually, Rosebud, but not tonight. Tonight is for getting to know each other better."

He loved the way she sighed and how her shoulders dropped as if she were disappointed. "Okay."

He patted the top of her car. "Follow me, Little girl." As he shut her door and headed toward his own car in the next row, he had to concentrate hard to keep from adjusting his cock.

She'd made him hard. Harder than he remembered being in a long time. She was so perfect for him. He knew it deep in his bones.

A lot of Daddies he knew had said they'd known the moment they found their Little girls. Now he understood. Rose was the one. It might take some time to convince her, but he was certain.

As he climbed into his SUV, he couldn't keep from smiling. He sure hoped it wouldn't take very many days to convince Rose to be his in every way because his entire body was humming at the suggestion of making love to her.

He also liked the fact that she'd said "make love" instead of "sex" because he most certainly intended to make long, slow, tender love to his sweet Little girl when they got to that stage of their relationship.

Adam was glad he hadn't lost Rose on the drive. He'd led her to the bank first so she could drop off her deposit and then his home, keeping her in his rearview mirror the entire time.

Finally, he would get to be alone with her. Granted, they'd shared some intimate moments sort of alone in her shop the past few nights, but it wasn't the same. Anyone could have walked up at any time. In fact, the night watchman had done exactly that.

After opening the garage, he pulled in, shut off the engine, and hopped down from his SUV.

Rose parked behind him in the driveway and opened her car door before he could reach her. She must have been distracted or flustered though because she turned to get out and got pulled up short, the seatbelt still wrapped across her chest.

"Oops." She giggled as she twisted to unbuckle the belt before facing him.

He loved when she was discombobulated and he reached

out to take her hand in his. The urge to kiss her again before shutting the door or leading her inside was strong, but he tamped it down. He could wait one more minute.

Something caught his eye in the passenger seat. "You brought Ruff?"

She turned around and looked back inside as if just now remembering her small stuffed friend. "Ruff wanted to spend some time with us. He gets lonely when he's by himself. Would it be okay if he came inside?"

"Of course. We certainly can't leave him out here. He'd be scared in the dark. Besides, he should get a tour of the house with you. If not, we'd have to repeat the tour another night."

The broad smile Rose gave him made every moment of this banter worthwhile. She continued to stare at him for several seconds, her smile growing as if she enjoyed their exchange every bit as much as he did.

Finally, she twisted around, leaned into the car, and snatched both the beagle and her purse. She tucked the small dog under one arm so he was facing out and his line of sight wasn't blocked. "We're ready for the tour."

Adam took her other hand in his and led her into the garage. Her small, soft fingers felt perfect in his. After pushing the button to shut the garage door, he led her into the kitchen and flipped on the lights.

"Tour starts with the kitchen," he informed her. As he pointed around, he gave her unnecessary information. "Fridge, stove, oven, counter, island, table, chairs..."

She giggled. "Ruff thinks you're silly."

"Ruff is a smart dog." He released her hand long enough to take her purse and set it on the corner of the counter before threading their fingers together this time and leading her deeper into the house.

"Your house is amazing, and so big," she stated as she let her gaze wander all over this space. "Modern."

"I spent months house hunting before I bought this place.

It's been several years, but I couldn't decide if I wanted something old and quaint or new and modern. In the end, modern won out, mostly because this one had everything I wanted, and it was available."

"What things did you want in a home?" she asked as he led her toward the front of the house.

"I wanted a place where my future Little girl could be happy, most importantly."

She gasped and looked up at him. "You were thinking of your future Little?"

"Yep." Instead of elaborating, Adam pointed out the rooms inside the front door. "Living room on this side." He nodded toward the right. "And my office is over here."

She stepped partway into the office. "Wow. You have a lot of books. It's more like a library."

"I love to read."

"I do too." She flashed him one of her sexy smiles.

He gave her hand a tug and led her deeper into the room. When he reached the sitting area around the fireplace, he stroked the back of the loveseat. "When I bought this couch, I pictured sitting in it with the perfect Little girl long into our old age. The fire blazing in front of us to keep us warm. My Little girl cradled in my lap or lying next to me with her head on my thigh, both of us reading."

"I love that," she murmured. "I can't believe I'm here and you think I'm your Little girl."

"I *know* you're mine, Rosebud." He lifted her hand to his lips and kissed her knuckles. It took great restraint to stop at that, to lower her fingers and lead her out of the office.

Adam's mind was racing with new visions of the future. The Little girl he'd always dreamed of having was in his home, in the flesh. She was adding a face and a body to his imagination.

Her cute bob would spread out across his thigh where he

could run his fingers through the locks. She would purr softly, contentedly, as she curled against him.

He hoped sometimes she would let him lure her into a very young age, leaning back in his lap, taking a bottle, wearing footed pajamas.

He needed to slow down, not let his imagination get so carried away. After all, he just met her a few days ago and this was the first time she was in his home. He knew though. She was his.

"Want to see the upstairs?" he encouraged to take his mind off her lips and the way she chewed on them when she was nervous.

"Yes." She adjusted Ruff under her arm. Such a darling sweet Little girl.

He led her upstairs next, pointing out the guest rooms and guest bath before entering the master bedroom.

Rose gasped. "It's so big. It's bigger than my whole apartment. Where do all those doors lead?" She pointed at each of them.

Adam stepped behind her and set his hands on her shoulders, mostly because he wanted to be closer to her. He angled her toward the left and slowly spun her clockwise, pointing out each room as they turned. "Bathroom, closet. closet. And lastly, the nursery."

He was glad he had his hands on her so he could feel her startle as she twisted her head to look at him. "Nursery? Do you have a baby?"

He chuckled, shaking his head. "Not for a small baby, Rosebud. The nursery is for you. It's for an adult Little."

She gasped, eyes wide yet again. "For me?"

"Yep. I've slowly decorated it for years, always hoping to find my Little girl. It's yours. Of course, I couldn't know what décor you might prefer or what colors you might like, so we'll make changes to suit your tastes. Want to see it?"

She stared at him, chewing on that lip again for several

seconds before speaking. "This is so fast, and I've never had a nursery before. I know some other Littles have them, but I don't even know what would be in a nursery."

"Would you like to see it?" he asked again, lifting a brow. "You don't have to if you're not ready."

She slowly nodded and swallowed hard, visibly gathering her courage. "I think I'm ready."

"Do you think you could also try calling me Daddy and see how it feels coming off your tongue?" he proposed.

She licked her full lips this time. "Maybe... Daddy." Her cheeks pinkened with embarrassment, but the corners of her eyes crinkled as she smiled.

"I like the sound of that, Rosebud. Let's check it out." He guided her forward until they reached the special room attached to the master bedroom. Opening the door, he held his breath. This was important to him. He wanted her to love the room.

Rose stepped inside tentatively and looked around, leaving him behind.

He stayed in the doorway, releasing her shoulders to let her explore. He held his breath and watched her closely, not wanting to miss any of her expressions.

Unfortunately, she faced away from him, not giving him a single hint about what she was thinking. She walked slowly, adorably, making sure Ruff could also see every detail.

She circled from the right to the left, taking in the adult-sized daybed that could convert into a crib first. She stroked the mahogany wood frame before moving on to the rocking chair, the bookshelf, the toy chest, the dresser, and finally, the changing table.

She lingered several heart-stopping seconds next to that last piece of furniture before turning to face him. "How young do you want your Little girl to be?" she asked, hesitation in her voice.

"We'll figure that out together, Rosebud, but it's good for

Little girls to have some time in a very Little space occasionally. It helps them recharge."

"I've never thought about practicing a younger age play," she hedged, chewing on that lip again.

He approached her and cupped her face, tipping her head back to look into her deep, inquisitive, curious eyes. "There's no rush, Rosebud. When you're ready, we'll explore every aspect of age play. For now, I don't want you to worry about it. Okay?"

She nodded subtly. "Yes, Daddy."

His cock throbbed in his pants when she called him Daddy, unprompted this time. "Good girl. Now, I'd really like to kiss you again. May I?"

Her smile widened. "I'd like that." She surprised him when she twisted around and set Ruff on the changing table before facing Adam again. Wrapping her arms around him, she tipped her head back.

He slid his hands up her back and hugged her tight before lowering his lips to hers and kissing her.

It started out innocent enough, but seconds later, he eased his hand to the back of her neck and guided her to tip her head to one side, deepening the kiss. She tasted like...bubble gum, and he didn't hesitate to stroke the inside of her mouth before gently sucking on her tongue.

Damn, she made him want her. He wished he could swing her up onto the changing table, strap her down for safety, and peel her clothes off. He wanted to see all of her, taste her, make her writhe on the table until she was panting and begging him to let her come.

They were both panting when he finally broke the kiss.

"Wow," Rose murmured. She was flushed, her cheeks rosy, her lips swollen and wet.

"Yeah, wow. It's going to be hard to resist you, Little girl."

"I'm not sure I want you to, Adam." Her voice was husky, sexy, tempting. And the way she said his name. His real name...

It bore into him and made him wish for things that were inappropriate. It was too soon.

"Another time, Little one."

Damn, he was hard though, and there was no way to hide that fact from her. She could surely feel his length pressing against her tummy.

Chapter Six

Rose had never felt even half what she'd been feeling from the moment she'd met Adam three days ago. She was having trouble remembering how to breathe as he rubbed her back and stared down at her.

When he set his forehead against hers, apparently trying to catch his own breath too, she sighed contentedly. This was really happening. After years of thinking she might never find a Daddy of her own, she was in Adam's house—in his nursery, no less—feeling all the warm and fuzzy thoughts she'd only ever had when reading her favorite romance novels.

It felt like she was actually inside one of her books. Surely real life couldn't be so titillating. She was pretty sure this was real though. Unless Adam was hiding an ugly side, he seemed to be the real deal. Her Daddy.

The timing sucked. She'd just opened a business. She worked long hours. She was going to be exhausted tomorrow after spending this time with him. It was late. She never stayed up this late.

Plus, all her days in the near future were going to look like this—long hours at Stuff-It followed by dropping into bed exhausted. In addition, it was the holidays. She had more business than usual with Christmas approaching.

"Where did your mind go, Little girl? You suddenly look sad." He cupped her shoulders and leaned back to examine her face, his brow furrowed.

"I just remembered all my real-life demands and how I don't have time to be your Little girl right now," she pointed out sadly.

He cupped her face. "Rosebud, you already are my Little girl. I know you're busy, but we'll figure it out together. Promise me you'll keep an open mind. I'll come help you close up at night and we'll spend late evenings together like tonight. We can have mornings too. I'll make sure I don't have early meetings for a while so I can be with you until you go to work as often as I can."

He sounded so sure they could make this work. It scared her a bit because she didn't have his confidence. She couldn't visualize how she could possibly spend evenings and mornings with him without losing sleep and growing increasingly more exhausted. "I'll fall asleep at the wheel if I leave here at midnight and get up early to go out to breakfast more than one day," she pointed out.

He kissed her briefly. "Then we'll cut out the wheel altogether," he proposed, confusing her.

"I'm pretty sure it would be worse if I started walking home," she teased.

"Stay here," he blurted. "Stay here with me. You can sleep in your nursery until you're ready to move to my bed. I'll make sure you get eight hours. I'll even tuck you in and make you breakfast so you head to work each day well rested and fed."

She dug her teeth into her bottom lip. Was he serious?

He kept talking. "I mean it, Rosebud. I know it's fast, but what can it hurt? I'm not asking you to let me into your body yet. I'm asking you to let me show you what a fantastic Daddy I can be. Let me take care of you when you're not working. Give me all your free time."

She glanced to the side, eyeing the gorgeous inviting daybed, not overlooking the railing that could be lifted to turn it into a crib. This was madness though. "I hardly know you."

"There's no better way to decide if I'm the sort of Daddy you want to know better than anyone alive for the rest of your life than to stay at my house while we feel each other out."

It was a crazy idea. What would people think? Then again, who would even know? She didn't have super close friends in town who would judge her. What would be the harm in taking him up on his offer?

He waited patiently.

"Okay, Daddy," she finally agreed. "I would need to get some things though. When do you want to start this experiment?"

He smiled broadly. "Three days ago, but I don't have a time machine, so we'll have to start today. I bet I can find something for you to wear to bed and you can swing by your apartment in the morning to change and pack a few things."

It sounded so easy. It sounded scary too. "Sometimes I still have work to do even when I'm not at the mall," she warned. "Social media. Marketing plans. Placing inventory orders. Owning a business is a lot at first."

"I'll help you."

"Don't you have your own full plate running the gumball factory?"

"I can slack off for a while. I have amazing staff. They'll ensure the company runs smoothly while I spend some time with my Little girl," he explained. He gave her a squeeze. "Let's get something in you. I bet you missed dinner again."

She sighed. "I did, but now I'm over it. It's too late. If I eat now, I'll have trouble sleeping."

He frowned. "You can't go without food, Rosebud. How

about if I make you a protein shake? It won't be so hard on your tummy while you sleep."

She smiled. "That would work."

"I make an amazing protein shake. It's my own secret recipe. You'll love it."

"I can't wait." She was still nervous, but she felt lighter as he led her back downstairs and into the kitchen. The worst thing that could happen would be they decided they weren't compatible and went their separate ways. Maybe it was wise to jump all in at once. Maybe everyone should do it. At least it would only take days instead of weeks or months to determine they weren't going to make it as a couple.

Rose watched from a stool at the island as her Daddy blended all sorts of yummy things in the blender for her. When he was done, he turned toward her. "I can put this in a regular cup, a sippy cup, or a bottle. Would you like to try taking a bottle? I'd love to rock you in my lap while you eat. I think you'll enjoy it. It's so intimate."

She hesitated. "Hmmm. Okay, but just the bottle. I'm not ready for any of the other things Babies use."

"Deal. Just the bottle for tonight." He poured it into a large adult-sized bottle and screwed the lid on. The nipple was also large. Just her size, she supposed. "Ready?"

She yawned. "So tired, Daddy."

"Then let's get you fed and into bed." He nodded over his shoulder and she followed him back toward the stairs and up to the nursery. "How about you go potty, and we'll put jammies on you first so all we'll need to do after the bottle is brush your teeth before you drift into sleep?"

She smiled. "Do you have jammies?"

"Yep. A Daddy is always prepared." He opened a drawer on the dresser and pulled out something soft and pink and fluffy. When he held it up, she grinned. It was the cutest pair of bunny-footed pajamas with a zipper up the front. When he spun it around, she giggled. There was even a cotton tail at the butt, flat enough that it wouldn't annoy her if she were to lie on it. He tugged the tag off and tossed it in the trash.

"I can't believe you even have jammies."

He shrugged. "I've been collecting stuff for years, hoping and waiting. Now you're here. I'm glad these are your size." He pointed toward the door. "Go potty, and then we'll get you changed."

She hesitated. "Should I take the jammies with me and change in the bathroom?"

"I'd rather you let Daddy change you, Rosebud. I promise I won't rush you and turn it into anything sexual tonight."

She bit her lip again and released it. "I'm not sure that's possible. I'd kind of prefer you did turn it into something sexual," she hedged. She hadn't been the one to put the kibosh on having sex. That had been all him.

"We'll see, Little girl. Go potty," he ordered in a firmer voice. "I'm not taking off any clothes myself, but if you're good and you do as Daddy says, maybe I'll explore your sweet Little body while I change you."

Her pussy clenched at the idea and she grinned.

He lifted a brow and glanced at the open door.

She spun around and raced toward the bathroom, realizing he meant business. She sure didn't want him to change his mind. She might not fully trust this relationship could honestly last for a lifetime after three days of lusting after him day and night, but she wasn't a prude. She'd love for him to take her to his bed. He seemed intent on digging his heels in on that subject. However, he had offered to explore her body, and she wasn't going to look a gift horse in the mouth.

She quickly peed and washed her hands, returning to her Daddy in minutes.

He was sitting on the edge of the daybed when she arrived, and she hurried over to him with her hands on the hem of her shirt, ready to pull it off.

As she kicked off her shoes, he stopped her from lifting her work T-shirt over her head. "Slow down, Little girl. Let Daddy take care of you. What's the fun in having a Daddy if you aren't going to let him see to your needs?"

She dropped her hands. It was too late for her shoes. They were already off. But she could let him do the rest. In fact, she was excited by the proposition. "No one has ever changed my clothes before," she informed him.

"That pleases me, Rosebud. I'm glad I'll be the first Daddy to undress you." He set his hands on her hips and pulled her between his legs before lifting her shirt slowly over her head.

She held her breath as his gaze roamed over her torso. She didn't have issues with her body, but it was always unnerving when someone else saw her naked for the first time. Granted, only two other people had ever seen her naked, and it had been a long time.

Adam spread his palms on the bare skin of her waist and held her steady before sliding them up around to her back and unfastening her bra. As he let it fall down her arms to set it aside, his breath hitched.

She watched his expression. Did he like what he saw?

His palms came back to her waist and slid up until he thumbed first the undersides of her breasts and then her nipples.

She gasped. Goosebumps rose all over her skin. She'd never felt this sexy, this worshiped.

Finally, he spoke in a soft, deep voice. "You are the prettiest Little girl I've ever seen, Rosebud. I'm so humbled you agreed to stay and that you're trusting me to see to your needs."

She swallowed. The word *needs* had so many meanings right now. She had a lot of needs.

His hands eased down to her jeans next, and he took his time releasing the button and lowering the zipper.

She hadn't really imagined he would end up seeing her undergarments tonight, so she hadn't worn sexy lingerie. The white panties and bra were ordinary and plain. "I should have worn something black and lacy," she murmured.

He shook his head as he lowered her jeans down her legs. "No. The white is precious. It suits you. When you're home, I'll pick your panties for you anyway, and Little girls don't wear bras when they're in Little space."

She flinched. "No bras?" She had modest boobs, but she still didn't go without a bra unless she was sleeping.

"Nope." He discarded her jeans and lifted one foot at a time to remove her socks next. As he did so, she grabbed his shoulders. She loved the feel of his hands even on her ankles and feet.

Finally, she was naked except for her panties and embarrassed to realize she wished he would take those off too, but she would never be bold enough to suggest such a thing. Besides, she was feeling much Littler as he cared for her, and with that came her shyer side. Any boldness she had earlier disappeared as she slid into deep Little space.

His hands smoothed up her body. "So soft," he muttered. "So pretty."

She bit her lip hard, her heart racing. Her panties were soaked. Her nipples were hard points. She'd never once had an orgasm with a man, but suddenly she thought she might come just standing here. She didn't even need him to touch her intimately. His reverent gaze alone was enough to make her pussy clench and her breath hitch.

"Adam…" She moaned his name as she grew restless from waiting.

"Let me look at you, Rosebud. I'll only get to see you naked for the first time once. I want to remember every detail. I want to remember the way your breath hitches and how your pretty, rose-colored nipples pucker for me. How you're shifting your weight from foot to foot. The scent of your arousal. Are your panties wet, Rose?"

She nodded. They were soaked.

"I want to lay you down on this bed and touch you gently until you come for me. Is that okay?"

She nodded again. She couldn't think straight, but she knew to the core of her being that was what she wanted. All of it. She was so aroused, she thought she might even succeed in coming for him, but she didn't want him to have expectations she might not meet.

She licked her lips. "I, uh…"

"What, Little Rosebud? You can tell me anything. Do you want me to stop?"

She shook her head. "No. I just… Uh… I've never had an orgasm in front of someone before. I don't want you to be disappointed if I don't come."

His eyes widened and then he smiled. "Thank you for sharing with me, Rose. I don't want you to worry about reaching orgasm. Just relax and enjoy yourself. If you don't come, we'll try again another time."

She nodded, relaxing further now that she didn't have to worry about him being disappointed or having his ego damaged.

Adam stood, lifted her off the floor, and gently laid her on the daybed so her legs were hanging off the sides and she was looking up at him.

When he set his palms on either side of her and leaned over to reverently kiss her nipple, she arched and moaned. *Jesus, maybe I can come from his touch.*

Chapter Seven

Adam couldn't believe this sweet woman was here in his home, nearly naked, splayed out on the bed he hoped she would spend time in often for the rest of her life.

She was panting and squirming with need. It seemed unfathomable that she wouldn't orgasm for him. He was confident she would, but he didn't say so because there was no sense adding to her concern. He would show her what it meant to be thoroughly loved with his hands and his mouth until she didn't know up from down and couldn't catch her breath.

"Panties off, Little girl. Push your hips up for Daddy," he directed and hooked his fingers into the sides of the plain white panties that enchanted him with their simplicity.

He eased them over her hips and down her legs. Adam could see that the crotch was wet with her juices as she squirmed on the bed to help him. When he removed them over her feet, he lifted the soft fabric to his nose and inhaled deeply as he held her gaze. Adam loved seeing her eyes cloud with arousal as she watched him enjoy her scent.

"So sweet, Rosebud."

After tucking the panties into his pocket, Adam ran a hand down her jawline to cup her throat. He watched her reaction closely and loved the flare of heat in her eyes. She enjoyed being held in place. As he suspected, she was his perfect match.

"Good girl, Rosebud. Daddy thinks you are delectable." He released his hand and trailed his fingertips over her collarbone and down the center of her torso to pause between her full breasts. Adam stroked the side of his thumb over the swell of one sweet mound and watched her shiver.

Sliding his fingers around the underside of one breast, Adam cupped her soft globe and tweaked her nipple between his thumb and finger. He loved how she jolted, pressing herself against his palm. Holding her gaze, he bent over her body and captured that taut peak between his lips.

"Mmm." He treasured that first intimate taste of her and knew it would not be enough. Adam wouldn't pleasure her orally tonight until they'd had a talk about her limits and health. That wouldn't deter him from helping her orgasm on his fingers.

Releasing her nipple with a pop of suction, Adam propped himself onto one elbow so he could watch her. When Rose bit her lower lip, he pressed a kiss to her mouth, seducing her as his fingers trailed over her softly curved abdomen to the silken curls he'd unveiled. Adam tugged her adult curls gently as a warning before sliding his fingertips into her soaked pink folds.

He whispered against her lips, "You are so wet, Little girl. I think you like my touch."

She nodded a wee bit before whispering, "I don't know if I can come. I have trouble..." Her admission grew quieter until obviously she ran out of courage.

Adam loved the sweet flood of color on her cheeks. His heart swelled in his chest as he treasured each delectable reaction she showed him. Running his fingers through her wetness, he traced her opening before circling that tight bud that topped her slit.

"Does it feel good if I touch you here, Rosebud?" he asked.

She nodded and looked away as if embarrassed.

"Keep your eyes on Daddy, honey. I need to see all your reactions. No hiding from Daddy."

"O-Okay," she promised as her gaze meshed with his immediately.

"That's my sweet girl," he praised as he softly tapped the tight nerve bundle. Adam saw her inhale sharply and noted her reaction. Shifting his thumb over the small nub, he continued to tantalize it as he rotated his hand to press two fingers against her wet opening. Without warning, he pressed them completely inside her.

"Ah!" she cried, lifting her hips up toward him as if to advance his touch further inside.

Adam held her to the mattress with a firm hand spanning her tummy. Again, her eyes glazed slightly in reaction to his control over her. He lowered his lips back to her nipple and sucked it into his mouth. Lashing the peak with his tongue, he stroked his fingers in and out of her body slowly as he searched for those pleasurable trigger spots deep inside her.

"Please," she begged as her body wiggled underneath his control.

He could feel shimmers of contractions around his fingers. His Little girl wanted to come but was resisting. She'd admitted she had trouble climaxing. Adam suspected she was thinking too hard, worrying about whether she'd make it there, and not allowing herself to simply feel. Tightening his teeth around the tight peak in his mouth, he bit her gently—just a small hint of pain. Her gasp of reaction preceded a long moan of pleasure as his distraction worked perfectly. Rose's body tightened around his fingers as she wiggled delectably.

"Good girl."

He gathered her beautiful body close to him and scooped Rose up in his arms. Holding her on his lap, Adam whispered sweet words and compliments as he rocked Rose slowly on the daybed. His Little girl clung to him as she recovered from her orgasm.

Finally, she peeked up at him. "I can't believe you made me feel so good. I never..."

When her voice trailed away, Adam pressed a soft kiss to her lips. "You needed to find your Daddy. I'm here now, and I'm going to help you feel special in all sorts of ways."

"I like this way," she rushed to assure him.

"I'm glad. I like watching you as well."

"Will you make love to me?"

"Not tonight. You're too sleepy. Do you need to potty again before Daddy tucks you into your jammies?" he asked.

When she nodded, he helped her stand and sent her to the bathroom with a firm pat on her cute bottom. To her surprise, he followed her.

"I can use the restroom by myself," she told him quickly.

"You potty. Daddy will take care of everything else."

Embarrassed, she sat down as he deliberately didn't watch her. Adam busied himself with opening the door to the linen closet and selecting a soft washcloth. He ran the water until it was warm. When she popped up and flushed the toilet, he wet the cloth.

"Lean over the vanity and spread your legs, Rosebud."

Hesitantly, she followed his directions. Rose looked over her shoulder at him several times to make sure she was doing what he wished. When she settled into place, he rubbed a hand over her back.

"A bit wider, please, Little girl," he requested and waited for her to spread her legs farther apart.

When she moved into the position he desired, Adam pressed a firm hand on her back to tether her in place and carefully wiped away the remnants of her pleasure from her inner thighs and those pink folds. He took care to also clean between her buttocks and watched a blush cover her cheeks until she hid her face in her hands. Touching her intimately turned her on.

I'll need to explore that more.

Pushing future promises away, he dried her skin and held

Rose's hand to lead her back to the nursery. In just a few minutes, he had her dressed and settled in his lap. He leaned her back and tapped her lips with the bottle. It was late, and she was tired, but he didn't like the idea of his Little girl going without meals. One of his top priorities was going to be feeding her balanced meals.

He smiled as she accepted the bottle without fussing. She started to drift off several times, but he jiggled the nipple to encourage her to finish. She sighed so contentedly when the bottle was empty, and he quickly tucked her into bed with Ruff in her arms. He wasn't fond of skipping teeth brushing, but he'd make an exception tonight. Her sleep was important. Skipping one night of brushing wasn't going to land her at the dentist.

She struggled to keep her eyes open as he grabbed a book of fairy tales from the toy chest and sat on the nearby rocking chair.

He watched her fight to stay awake while he read to her, but she slowly gave in to her exhaustion. Adam sat in the chair for a long time watching her. Every single detail of his Little girl enchanted him. He didn't want to miss anything. Finally, he forced himself to stand and go take a shower.

The next morning, he tiptoed into the nursery. Rose lay on her side with Ruff tucked under her chin. He knelt by the bed and whispered, "Sweet Rosebud, Daddy's sorry. It's time to wake up for breakfast."

"I don't want to wake up, Daddy," Rose protested sleepily. She squeezed her eyelids shut as if she could shut him out completely.

"You told me when we met that you were a morning person." He chuckled as he pulled the covers off. Perhaps that only applied to nights when she wasn't sleep deprived.

"No," she snapped and let go of Ruff to grab at the covers.

"Little girl," he warned, thwarting her attempts to snuggle back under the comforter.

She stared up at him and wrinkled her nose in anger. "You don't get to tell me when to wake up."

"Oh, Little girl. Your Daddy definitely has that right."

"Maybe you're not my Daddy," she volleyed back at him.

"The moment you came around my fingers there was no turning back. You are mine, Little girl. Your pleasure sealed that fact."

When she continued to look at him with a stubborn expression, Adam calmy removed her fingers from the covers and whisked the blankets down to the end of the bed, discovering that the front of her pajamas was completely unzipped. He plucked her out of bed and stood her in front of him. The look of surprise on her face could have made him laugh but he schooled his expression to look at her very seriously. He held her hands behind her back with one of his when she tried to cover up the portion of her body revealed by her gaping sleeper.

"Rose, Little girls who misbehave earn consequences." He watched her closely to see how she would respond to the idea of being punished. When her breath hitched and she squeezed her legs together, he knew what she needed. "You've earned your first consequence." He quickly tugged her one-piece bunny pajamas over her arms. Adam held her hands to prevent her from grabbing the material and allowed the sleeper to drop to the floor around her ankles.

"You can't spank me," she complained without enough umph behind her words. She was curious.

"I can and will when you're naughty. You can either cooperate or I will take your temperature to make sure you're not acting up because you don't feel well. Then if you don't have a fever, I'll add five more swats to the ten you've already earned."

He watched her think. She opened her mouth as if inviting the thermometer. Slowly, he shook his head and moved one hand behind her to pat her bottom. "Little girls have their temperatures taken here."

"In my bottom?" she gasped, but she also squirmed and clenched her bottom. Her cheeks were pink. Her breathing was erratic. Her nipples were hard points.

Adam saw the bluster dissolve from her face. "Would you like to cooperate or keep being naughty?"

"I'm sorry. I was asleep," she said quickly to excuse her behavior.

"I'll remember that as I'm spanking you."

"You're still going to spank me? But that's not fair!"

"Did you follow Daddy's instructions?" he asked.

"No, but—"

Adam interrupted her excuse. "Did you talk nicely to Daddy?"

This time she shook her head and dropped her chin to look at the floor.

"Did you lie, denying that I'm your Daddy?"

She nodded and her head drooped a bit lower.

"Do you deserve a spanking?"

Profound silence followed. Finally, she whispered, "Yes. I'm sorry, Daddy."

"That's my good Little girl. Let's wipe away your naughtiness. Lie over my lap," he instructed as he helped her move into position.

When her bottom pointed upward, he rubbed the cool flesh lightly, enjoying her shivers that he knew didn't come from being cold. They were pure anticipation. "Are you ready for me to spank you, Rose?"

"Yes, Daddy." Her voice was low and definitely tinged with something other than regret.

Immediately, Adam smacked her bottom sharply. Taking care not to use too much force, Adam watched a pink handprint form on her pale skin. He wanted her to remember this but not be bruised by his correction. Quickly, he applied several more to her exposed skin.

As she squirmed on his legs, Rose's legs parted to reveal shiny juices beginning to coat her inner thighs. She remained quiet. Adam wanted her to remember this first spanking. He needed to know how far to push her. Continuing to pepper her skin with swats, Adam listened carefully.

When he heard that first sob, Adam asked, "Do you want to apologize to Daddy for your behavior?"

"Y-yes!" she stuttered. "I'm sorry. I won't be rude again in the morning. I promise."

Without saying a word, Adam lifted her and sat her hot bottom on his hard thigh as he wrapped his arms around her. "Let's have a redo of the morning."

"How do we do that?"

"Just like this. Good morning, Rosebud. I'm afraid it's time to get up."

She stared at him for a fraction of a second before answering, "Hi, Daddy."

"Did you sleep well?"

"Yes. I didn't wake up once," she assured him.

He lifted a brow, wondering if she would lie to him again. "Did you touch yourself after your orgasm?"

She shook her head rapidly, denying his question without saying anything.

"When I ask you a question, I want you to answer with words, Rose. Did you touch yourself after your orgasm last night?"

Instantly, she shook her head to deny him again. "No, Daddy. I don't remember unzipping my jammies, but I do remember being hot. I must have been trying to cool off."

He smoothed one hand up one of her creamy white thighs to stroke his fingers through the slick juices that gathered there. "It feels like you've been playing."

"No, Daddy. I didn't. I just... I just got excited when you spanked me."

"Why?" Adam continued to stroke her intimately, searching for those sensitive trigger points he'd memorized last night.

She looked at him in shock for several seconds as she tried not to respond. When he slid two fingers into her pussy, Rose blurted, "It was the spanking. It made me wet."

"Thank you for telling me, Little girl. You deserve a reward for admitting the truth and taking your spanking so well, don't you?" Adam suggested, stroking her intimately.

"A re-reward?" she stuttered.

"Let's see if Daddy can make you come this morning. That should turn your morning grouchies to sweetness for the day." He abandoned his touch for a few seconds to press her knees apart. "Stay like this. Watch Daddy make you feel good."

He smiled as she stared at his hands moving between her thighs. Already, he could feel small contractions around his inserted fingers. He dipped a fingertip of his free hand into her slick juices and raised it to paint over her mouth. "Lick your lips, Little girl. Does your excitement taste as good as I anticipate it will?"

Her soft moan of enjoyment answered him as the pink tip of her tongue flicked outside. Rose's attention didn't waver from the intimate touches Adam lavished on her. He pressed hot fiery kisses to the curve of her neck and nibbled on her shoulders. When he felt her tight channel clinch around him, Adam pinched that small bundle of nerves. She screamed her climax into the room.

Chapter Eight

Rose had trouble meeting people's eyes at Stuff-It that morning. She was sure everyone could tell she'd been spanked and pleasured before coming to work. She could definitely feel her stinging bottom and the continual wetness between her thighs. It was impossible to wipe the memories of watching him stroke her.

Adam had sent her home to change clothes with a breakfast sandwich in her hand and a lunch sack for later. Her face heated as she remembered him having to change his slacks for a fresh pair because her juices had coated them. A picture of his erection pressing urgently against his boxer briefs when he changed made her panties wetter.

I want him so bad.

Rose had packed a bag with several days of clothes. She'd promised to return after work. Thank goodness it was busy. Time was moving quickly despite her anticipation. His texts throughout the day reassured her he wanted to be with her as much as she needed him.

Finally, she was able to close the shop and drive to his house. Adam met her on the driveway. He'd watched for her.

"Come in, Rosebud. I've missed you."

"I couldn't wait to get back here," she admitted and earned a scorching kiss.

When he lifted his head, she waved an arm toward the trunk to signal to him wordlessly that she'd stored something there as she pushed the button on her car remote to open it. Spotting the bag, he pressed a softer kiss to her lips before moving to grab it. Carrying it, Adam ushered her into the house. He led her directly upstairs to the nursery and placed her purse and the large bag on the foot of the bed, avoiding a small pile of clothing that already lay there.

"Let Daddy change your clothes to something more comfortable and then we'll eat some dinner." He stripped off her clothes, pressing kisses to her body as he unveiled her.

She watched him squeeze her wet panties in his hand. He would realize she'd been turned on all day. "It's your fault."

"I'll take responsibility for that," he said cheerfully as he added them to the neatly folded clothes he'd removed. Adam didn't dally but dressed her in the soft leggings and T-shirt that lay folded on the daybed she had slept on last night.

"Did you have more clothes in the drawer?" she asked curiously as she stroked over the material she wore. There was a line of lace at the bottom of the shirt, but it didn't scratch. She thought it was so pretty.

"I went out and bought these at lunch. How did Daddy do? Are you comfortable?"

"I love these. Thank you."

"You're very welcome, Rosebud. Ready to go eat? Do you like baked potato soup?" he asked.

"Yum," she answered.

"Me, too. I thought we could talk over dinner about what we both need from our relationship."

"Did I do something wrong?" Rose asked, holding her breath.

"Never. I want to make sure we're on the same wavelength. Did you bring Ruff?"

"He's in my purse."

Retrieving the puppy stuffie, she slid her hand into his and clung to her Daddy as he led her downstairs and to the kitchen table. Sitting down in the chair he indicated, Rose watched him ladle up a large bowl of soup and sprinkle bacon and cheese on top after asking her if she liked both on her soup.

"I can't eat that much," she rushed to tell him as he carried the large container to the table.

"We'll work on this together. Did you eat your lunch?" he asked.

"I didn't have a chance, but I'll eat it tomorrow," she promised.

"Make sure you take a break, Little girl. You don't want to get sick," Adam warned as he sat down next to her and placed the bowl between them.

"I will."

Her Daddy picked up one spoon and asked, "Do you need to share any medical information with me, Rose? I was screened last month for any sexually transmitted diseases and I'm clear."

"Oh!" The meaning of his question was definitely clear. "I'm clean, too. I was tested a couple of years ago but haven't been with anyone since."

"Then we can share one spoon." He dipped the utensil into the thick mixture before raising the steaming soup and blowing on it. "Try a small taste. Tell me if it's too hot and we need to let it cool."

Rose opened her mouth and let him feed her. The delicious concoction tasted phenomenal. "Mmm! It's perfect. You take a bite."

Adam followed her suggestion and waggled his eyebrows happily. "I didn't do too bad."

"You're a great cook," she enthused, leaning forward to let him feed her again.

"Why are your lips chapped, Little girl? Did you not drink enough water?"

Instantly, her face heated, and she knew her cheeks were bright red. "Do I have to tell you?" Rose looked down at the tabletop to avoid meeting his eyes.

"Yes." His hand under her chin raised her gaze to meet his. "No secrets between Little girls and their Daddies."

"I kept licking my lips. You put my..." Her voice died and she pleaded with her eyes that he'd understand.

"You enjoyed tasting your own flavor," he guessed.

She could only nod her head. When Adam leaned forward to kiss her, Rose puckered her lips in a silent invitation.

"Next time, I get to enjoy your juices," he informed her. His eyes gleamed with desire.

"Are you going to make love to me?" she whispered.

"Yes. The question is simply when. Let's eat our dinner first, hmmm?" he teased.

"Daddy!"

Adam laughed. The deep, masculine sound made her wiggle in her chair and hope she wouldn't leave a damp spot there when she stood up.

When they'd finished, Rose slouched back against her chair. His questions had been direct and personal, but she felt incredibly reassured that he cared so much about her that he wanted her to be safe. They'd talked about birth control and her sexual experience and fantasies. Rose had admitted more things to him than she'd actually figured out on her own.

Nothing she said had turned him off. In fact, his persistent erection pressing against his fly made her realize how turned on he was as well. She tried to cool down as he cleaned the kitchen and put away the leftovers, but the slight pause only raised her anticipation.

"Shall we go brush our teeth and go to bed, Rosebud?

Would you like to sleep with Daddy tonight or in your nursery?"

"Daddy," she whispered.

"Come on, Little girl." Adam offered her a hand and led her to the master bedroom.

Stopping in the bathroom, he put toothpaste on two toothbrushes. They each brushed their teeth. The innocent act seemed very intimate.

When Adam wet a washcloth, she blushed furiously again and then giggled when he cleaned her makeup off her face. That was definitely not what she expected.

"Are you thinking about Daddy wiping your pussy?" he asked.

"Yes."

"You might just be the death of me." Adam leaned over and lifted her up over his shoulder. He spanked her bottom as he carried her into the bedroom.

"Ouch!"

"I'm glad the sting stayed with you. Little girls learn how to behave when they have an ouchie bottom to remind them." Adam set her feet on the carpet next to the large bed and reached for the hem of her T-shirt.

"Are you going to spank me often?" she asked, her voice muffled by the material sliding over her head.

"Yes." He pulled her pants off and tugged back the covers. "Crawl in, Rosebud."

Stretching out on the crisp sheets, Rose rested her head on the pillow as she prepared to watch the show. Adam stripped off his shirt over his head. She loved the play of his muscles as he moved. When he eased the navy sweatpants over his erect cock, she almost choked on the suddenly thick air. Adam turned around to throw their clothes into the laundry hamper in the corner of his room, and she got an inspiring view of his ass.

Try to act cool!

He stalked toward her, holding her gaze.

Rose sucked in a breath and held it. She couldn't keep her eyes on his. They strayed lower, and lower, until she was staring at his impressive erection. She squirmed and scooted back a few inches.

She wasn't sure why she was nervous. There was no reason to be. She'd seen naked men before. She'd had sex. Why did this seem different?

Her breath hitched when he set his hands on the mattress and leaned toward her. "You can tell Daddy no, Rosebud. You know that, right?"

She licked her lips and shook her head. "I want to make love with you, Daddy."

He smiled, a brilliant smile that made his eyes light up and the corners crinkle. "You look very nervous, Rose." He lifted a knee onto the bed and then the other, crawling toward her, then over her.

She swallowed. "I can be nervous and want this at the same time," she informed him.

"You sure can, Rosebud." He bent over her and kissed her lips gently. No other part of him was touching her.

She moaned into his mouth, glad for the distraction. Adam was an amazing kisser. Every time he took her lips, she melted. He had a way of calming her and exciting her at the same time.

When he finally released her, she was panting. "You okay, Rosebud?"

She nodded. "Yes, Daddy."

"I'm going to taste you now," he warned.

She bit her bottom lip, not quite sure what he meant.

"*All* of you," he informed her. "Every inch."

Oh. Ohhh.

He kissed her lips one more time and then crawled down her body several inches and lowered his gaze to her chest. As he bent slowly toward one globe, he whispered, "Prettiest Little girl ever."

His breath hit her nipple, making her squirm as it stiffened.

He continued to hover, which made her pulse pick up. "Daddy…" Her voice surprised her. She sounded desperate. She *felt* desperate too.

"I want to take my time, Rosebud. Savor this experience."

She lifted her hands, thinking to wrap them around his neck and pull him closer.

Daddy stopped her with a shake of his head. "Keep your hands at your sides for now, Rosebud. Let Daddy explore."

"But…" She wanted to touch him as badly as he wanted to touch her.

"No buts, Little girl. Daddy's rule."

She shuddered, wondering if he would spank her if she touched him. Her face flushed at the thought. She'd enjoyed his first spanking. A bit too much probably.

When he leaned closer and intentionally blew against her nipple, she arched. A soft moan escaped. He wasn't even touching her and she felt like she was close to orgasm. So much for not being able to come with a man. Apparently those days were in the past. Her Daddy had super powers.

Finally, he closed the distance and sucked her nipple in between his lips. He immediately grazed it with his teeth, making her writhe. She had to fist her hands at her sides to keep from grabbing him. A part of her—the naughty part—wanted to reach for him just to test him.

By the time he stopped tormenting her nipple to switch to the other one, she was panting heavily. It was hard to stay still, but she was trying to be good. The act of obeying him made her even more aroused.

"Good girl," Daddy murmured as he released the second nipple with a slight pop. He slid farther down her body, finally touching more of her when he nestled a knee between hers. "Open for me, Rosebud."

She parted her legs, breathing heavily as he climbed between them. She felt so exposed. Needy. So hot.

After long seconds of staring at her most private parts,

Adam lowered his chest between her legs, parted her thighs with his palms, and dropped his lips to her sensitive skin.

She gasped when he kissed her mound. She'd known he would eventually do something like this because he'd said so, but nothing could have prepared her for the sensation. No previous partner had ever kissed her down there.

She was still wrapping her mind around Daddy's location between her thighs when he suddenly sealed his open mouth over her clit and sucked.

Rose cried out. It wasn't even intelligible. Just noise.

He thrust his tongue into her channel next, making her arch and whimper. Her brain was scrambled. She was shaking as she instantly detonated, her orgasm making her entire body tremble and pulse.

By the time he lifted his mouth, she was putty beneath him, and she cried out when he thrust two fingers into her. He held them deep, not moving as she adjusted to the sensation.

Nervous energy consumed her. "Please, may I touch you, Daddy?"

He smiled and nodded. "Yes, Rosebud. Such a good girl asking so nicely. You may touch me now."

Panting, she looked up at him. Rose wanted to be good for him. His praise meant everything. Unable to put her feelings into words, she wrapped her hands around his shoulders and pulled him toward her.

Adam slipped his fingers from her and leaned forward to kiss her fiercely. When he lifted his head, the dynamic man asked, "Are you ready to be mine, Little girl? I won't ever be able to let you go after we make love." He shook his head, before adding, "That's a complete lie. I can't let you go now, Rosebud. You're mine. My Little girl."

His words resonated inside her. She felt her lips curve in a smile. "I'm good with that," she confessed.

Adam ripped his gaze away from hers to lunge for the nightstand drawer. Opening it, he pulled out a small packet and rose to cage her underneath his body. Quickly, he opened it and started to roll the condom over his thick shaft.

When she reached up to help him, he brushed her hands away. "Let Daddy do it this time, Rosebud."

"Soon?" she asked. She wanted to touch him, feel his thickness and strength.

"Good girls get special privileges," he assured her.

Rose decided immediately that she could be better than she ever had. She linked her arms around his neck as he nestled the broad head of his cock against her opening. Rose had enjoyed the closeness of having sex before but realized in a flash of insight that this man she hadn't known for very long already meant more to her than anyone she'd ever dated. This definitely wasn't just sex to her.

Threading her fingers through his thick hair, Rose lifted her head to press her lips against his. The searing kiss that followed confirmed her feelings were reciprocated fully. She moaned into his mouth as Adam pressed himself into her body, filling her completely.

"Mmm," he hummed against her lips. "You feel amazing, Rosebud."

Words failed her. Her mind couldn't focus on anything other than the feel of his hard body against her and inside her. Adam filled her senses. Rose nestled her face in the hollow of his neck, trying to gather herself. She shouldn't be this enamored with him. His scent tantalized her—hot, spicy, and completely male. Tasting him with a flick of her tongue, Rose savored his salty skin.

"You're killing me, Little girl. Let's see how good you can be," he suggested.

Daring a peek at his face, Rose was relieved to see Adam's expression. Adoration and fierce need etched themselves on his face. She curled her fingers into his broad shoulders to cling to him as he withdrew. His brief pause at her entrance seemed like forever but she knew it only lasted a second at most. With a firm thrust, he filled her again, his thick shaft gliding over all the sensitive spots his fingers had teased previously. She lifted her hips to press him a fraction deeper, drawing a groan of delight from him.

"Wrap your legs around me," he ordered as his hand slid under her hips to support her.

Clinging to his body, Rose wiggled against him, rubbing herself against his pelvis. Those shivers of delight rekindled inside her as they moved against each other. His hand under her bottom raised her to meet each thrust. She scattered kisses against his chest.

Their skin grew slick as they moved together. The aroma of sex filled the air as her focus narrowed to a small bubble around them. Nothing else mattered. Nothing else existed.

Adam twisted his hips at the end of his next stroke. With a cry, Rose exploded around him, her body contracting as waves of pleasure flooded her. She realized Adam came with her as his body stiffened and pulsed.

"Damn, Little girl. You feel so good," Adam growled into her ear.

Panting as her orgasm coursed through her, Rose abandoned any self-consciousness. She couldn't hide any part of herself from him. Her Daddy.

"Such a pretty Little girl," he complimented as he resumed his strokes. "One more for me."

"I don't think I can," she whispered, overwhelmed by the sensations.

"You can. For me, Rosebud. One more," he coaxed.

On his next stroke inside, Adam shifted his position to kneel in front of her. He drew her body easily with him until she lay draped over his thighs. A gasp escaped from her lips as he also moved his supporting hand to stroke his fingers down the cleft of her buttocks. Delving inside, he circled one fingertip around her small entrance.

A shiver of forbidden delight coursed through her. "Daddy?" she whispered.

"Daddy will touch you everywhere, Rosebud," he assured her in a deep voice that revealed his desire.

Her reservations dissolved. He was in charge. Rose nodded and gripped his muscular forearms as he quickened his thrusts.

"Good girl," he praised once again.

She felt that fingertip scoop up her juices and then glide through her defenses to invade her so intimately. With a scream of completion, Rose abandoned herself to the eroticism of his touch. His rapid strokes inside her pushed the climax higher, thrilling her. She smiled when his shout filled the air.

He gathered her to his chest, hugging her so tightly she could feel his heart pounding against her. Rose treasured the closeness. He was hers. She pressed kisses to his skin, feeling closer to him than ever before.

When his breathing slowed, Adam lowered her gently to the pillows before following her down to rest on his side. After disposing of the condom, he pulled her closer and rolled to his back with her cuddled against his chest.

Loving the feel of his arms around her, Rose wanted to freeze this moment in time. Her body still hummed with the pleasure they had created between them. She'd never felt this close to anyone in her life.

Adam cupped her chin and lifted it so he could look into her eyes. "I know it's soon, Rosebud, but I want you to know that I love you. I'm never letting you go."

"I love you, too, Daddy."

His mouth crashed down onto hers, staking his claim on her with a fiery kiss that curled her toes with delight. Her heart seemed to swell in her chest with happiness. She'd found the man she'd dreamed of for so long.

Chapter Nine

Adam's alarm beeped softly in the morning, waking them. Rose stirred in the curve of his arm, tucked against his body. She felt his lips press gently against her sleep-rumpled hair.

"Morning, Little girl. I'm sorry to wake you up so early. I have a meeting this morning I can't miss. Would you like to nap a bit longer and I'll wake you up for breakfast?"

"Can I do that?" she asked, struggling to open her eyes fully.

"Sleep, Rosebud. Daddy will help you get up later." He rolled out of bed and tugged the covers back into place.

Nodding, she turned over onto her tummy and nestled in the warm spot he'd just vacated. She inhaled deeply, enjoying his lingering scent on the sheets. A caressing hand roamed the length of her spine and cupped her bottom. Rose smiled as he patted fondly, reminding her of his play.

Like she could forget that.

She heard him moving quietly around the room and into the attached master bathroom. The sound of water spraying followed, and she couldn't stop the smile that curved her lips once again when she heard him groan in delight. Rose could picture him standing under the showerhead, enjoying the warm deluge.

His lovemaking still reverberated inside her. Rose hadn't known she could feel that depth of emotion. Her steamy dreams had come true every time she blinked her eyes open in the darkness and discovered that he held her close throughout the night. She'd felt precious and protected from everything.

"Time to wake up, Little girl." A soft voice pulled her out of the deep sleep she'd drifted into. The bed dipped as someone sat down next to her.

Rose opened her eyes to meet Adam's tender gaze. "Hi," she whispered, shyly, trying to show him she could be pleasant in the morning.

"Hi, Rosebud. Can you wake up to have breakfast with Daddy?"

She nodded and rolled over before asking, "Is it time for me to go to work? I need to shower first."

"You have a couple of hours. How about if you eat and then make yourself at home after I go to work? I want you to feel comfortable here," he suggested.

"I love it here with you," she admitted.

"Good. Now out of bed, sleepy girl. I'd like you to wear one of Daddy's T-shirts so you don't get cold." He tugged the covers away.

She loved how his gaze turned steamy as he scanned her naked body. Rose couldn't help feeling beautiful when he looked at her like that. Raising her arms, she allowed him to help her into the large garment. Her arms got tangled in the fabric and she laughed as he rescued her from her soft prison. His delighted chuckle warmed her heart. Her Daddy was always so fun to be around.

"Look what I found," he celebrated as her left arm finally

emerged. "I'm going to have to practice dressing you more often."

"I'd like that," she agreed.

"So would I, Rosebud." He stood and helped her scoot out of bed. "Go potty and meet me in the kitchen."

When she didn't move immediately, Adam swatted her bottom smartly. The sting made her hop in the direction of the bathroom. Rubbing her derriere, Rose walked toward the bathroom but shot an admonishing look over her shoulder at him.

"Daddy's in charge," he reminded her with a stern look that made her school her expression.

It would be tough to always follow his directions. Her aching bladder reminded her he was correct. She needed to hurry to the bathroom. Scurrying forward, Rose peed before washing her face and hands. As she padded back through the bedroom, she snagged Ruff from the bed.

Before heading to the kitchen, she stopped in the doorway to the nursery and imagined herself living here all the time. She looked around, marveling that he'd created this for her. Whirling around in delight, she gave Ruff a giant bear hug and he, of course, returned it twofold.

"Rosebud?" Her Daddy's voice drifted to her.

"Coming!" Rose called out before scampering down the stairs to join him.

She grinned broadly as she slid into the seat he held out for her at the table. When her Daddy lifted the dish cover in front of her, she discovered he'd already filled a plate for her, piled with eggs, bacon, and toast that still steamed with heat. A sippy cup of milk sat at her place too. She set Ruff on the chair next to hers, making sure he could see her while she ate.

"Dig in, Rosebud. I want you to start eating healthier. I don't like you going to work on an empty stomach." He leaned over and lifted her chin to meet her gaze. "And you better eat that sandwich I made you today or I'll spank your bottom so hard you won't be able to sit this evening. Understood?"

"Yes, Daddy." She nodded rapidly. She would eat her lunch this time. He was right. Skipping meals only made it hard for her to concentrate in the afternoons. Plus, she got hangry.

He slid into the seat next to her and took a sip of coffee.

She realized hers was the only plate at the table. "Did you already eat, Daddy?"

"Yep." He nodded toward hers. "Start eating or Daddy's going to feed you myself," he warned.

She giggled. "I'm not sure that's a very good threat, Daddy. I like it when you feed me."

He chuckled and ruffled her hair. "Good. I like feeding you too. I'll be doing so often."

She sat up straighter and picked up her fork to stab into a bite of fluffy scrambled eggs. Flavor burst on her tongue. After she chewed and swallowed, she asked, "What did you put in the eggs? They're amazing!" She crunched into the bacon next.

He winked. "Daddy magic."

She eagerly cleaned her plate while he watched. And then she stared at his coffee. "May I have some coffee, Daddy?"

He bent forward and kissed her forehead. "Nope. I bet you've been living off caffeine for a while. I want you to try eating healthy and drinking healthy beverages like milk, juice, and water for a while. I bet you'll sleep better and have more energy."

She pouted, pushing out her lower lip. "I'm not sure I can work without coffee," she grumbled.

"Try it for Daddy. I bet you can do it." He reached for her tummy and tickled her. "We filled that belly with protein and whole grains. Those will give you more energy than a caffeine breakfast, Rosebud."

She sighed. "Okay. I'll try."

"Good girl." He stood and carried her dishes to the sink to rinse them and stick them in the dishwasher. When he was finished, he came back to her and stroked her cheek. "I'm sorry, I have to go to my meeting. Remember, it will take you about twenty minutes to get to the mall. Go get cleaned up and text me when you're safely out of the shower. Your bag is in the bedroom next to the dresser. I cleaned out a few drawers so you can store some clothes here. I'll unpack for you when I get home tonight."

"Thank you, Daddy."

"Come give me a kiss," he requested, opening his arms to her.

Rose leaped into his embrace and looped her arms around his neck. Eagerly, she pressed her lips against his and loved his response to her. Her Daddy was a very good kisser.

"I'll miss you," she whispered as he set her back on her feet.

"I'll text you during the day to see how you're doing. I know you're busy, but I'd like you to answer at least once today. Can you do that for me?"

"Yes, Daddy. I promise."

"Come back here after work. I want to hold you in my arms."

"I want that, too," she whispered.

With one last steamy kiss, Adam disappeared into the garage. He must have negotiated getting his SUV around her car as he had assured her he could do because he didn't come back.

Rose looked at the shiny new key on her keychain. He'd given her a key to his house so she could get back inside if she forgot something and needed to retrieve it after he'd left or to let herself in if he was delayed after work.

Scanning the open kitchen and family room, Rose marveled at his trust in her. She took another sip of the milk he'd poured for her and scowled. That wasn't going to wake her up. She needed a cup of coffee, no matter what her Daddy had told her. Rose was sure there had to be Littles who drank the hot, caffeinated beverage in the morning. They couldn't all drink milk.

She peeked out the garage door to make sure his car was actually gone. Nothing there. Coffee! Within a minute, she'd found a cup and added a coffee pod to the fancy maker. Leaning in, she inhaled the amazing aroma of the brew that dripped down. When the last burst of liquid streamed into her cup, Rose scooped it out and took a careful drink. *Yum!*

Already she felt more prepared to tackle the day. Tucking Ruff under her arm, Rose carried her caffeinated treasure upstairs. She settled Ruff on the bed and padded to the bathroom, taking another sip of coffee before setting it on the vanity. By the time she showered quickly, it would be the perfect temperature to savor.

After dawdling in the warm spray, Rose dressed quickly and added her normal touch of makeup. She caught a glimpse of the bag and thought about other things from home she needed to bring. Not bring from home, she corrected herself. Suddenly, her lonely apartment didn't feel like her home anymore. She wanted to be with Adam. He felt like home.

Remembering her Daddy said he'd made space in a few drawers for her, she shuffled over to the dresser and opened three drawers before she discovered the empty ones. She grinned as she realized he'd cleared out lower drawers for her. They would be easier to get to.

She was so excited to be staying here that she grabbed her bag and unpacked her things into two of the drawers. "There," she declared when she finished, clapping her hands together. She turned toward Ruff and cocked her head to one side. "Is this happening too fast, Ruff? I put my things in a drawer. That feels like a huge step."

Ruff simply smiled at her, so she assumed he was pleased with the arrangement. He liked Adam. She was sure of it. After all, Adam had been the one to ensure Ruff had a home and was loved. If it weren't for Adam, Ruff might still be an unstuffed pelt in the lonely store. No wonder Ruff was so happy.

Catching sight of the time, she ran to pick up her stuffie and dashed down the stairs to find her purse. As she locked the door and headed to her car, her phone buzzed. She jumped into her car before pulling it out to read the text.

Little girl, are you safe?

Quickly, she typed back to him.

Sorry! I forgot to text you. I promise I didn't slip and fall and hit my head in the shower. I'm perfectly fine and I'm headed to the store.

I'm glad you're safe. By the way, one.

There was no time to answer him. Rose needed to drive. She wondered what he meant by *one* and tried to set a mental reminder to herself to ask when she reached the mall. Speeding through the late rush-hour traffic, Rose forced herself to concentrate.

Arriving later than usual, Rose parked and hurried into the mall. Larisa waited for her at the door. "Sorry! The roads were completely at a standstill in several places." With that half-truth serving as her excuse, Rose unlocked the store and ushered Larisa inside.

Rose threw her purse into her office and jumped into action. It didn't take long for the two women working together to fill the cash register, restock a few items of clothing, and don their festive Santa hats. Immediately, she thought of the newest Little Cakes cupcakes. She should bring each of the employees one to sweeten their last payday before Christmas.

The day flew past. Rose glanced at the clock and knew that Adam's day at work had finished. She liked thinking about him at home waiting for her. Smiling, she turned back to wait on the next customer.

A couple of hours later, Larisa emerged from the back rooms with an armful of sacks to replenish the supplies before she left at the end of her shift. "I think your phone is buzzing in the office," she reported to Rose quietly.

"I'll call whoever it is back later," she assured Larisa and continued ringing up the next customer lined up in front of her.

When she had time to grab a bite of the sandwich that should have been lunch, Rose checked her phone and found a few worthless emails, two missed calls from Adam, and the messages—*Two* and *Three*.

Frazzled, she didn't have time to worry about the messages until she left the mall at the end of the night.

Several hours later after locking up, she found Adam lounging against her car. One of the teenage boys from the pack she greeted every night stood a short distance from the muscular man. Their body languages appeared tense as if it were a standoff.

Quickly, she called, "Hi! Is everything alright? Someone didn't hit my car, did they?"

"Do you know this man?" the teenager demanded.

"Yes—of course. This is my... my boyfriend," she filled in, hoping Adam would understand her using such a vanilla word to explain their relationship.

"Oh!" The teenager assessed her face and figure as if wondering if older people could actually date.

"Thank you for watching out for her," Adam commented, obviously unconcerned by the grilling he'd gotten after taking his position to wait for her at her car.

With a nod, the young man drifted back to his friends, looking back a few times to double-check that she was okay.

"Sorry," she said quickly.

"I'm glad he's keeping people you don't want to talk to away. That took a lot of courage to approach a grown man," Adam observed.

"I'm pretty sure he thinks I'm ancient," Rose marveled.

Adam dismissed that thought with a shake of his head. "You ready to head home, Rosebud?"

She nodded. "I'm exhausted. I felt like I was behind most of the day. Traffic was so thick on the way here that I barely made it to work before the store opened. Larisa was already waiting for me."

Daddy lifted a brow and stared at her. "Hmmm. Let's go home, Little girl." He took her keys from her, unlocked her car, and helped her into the driver's seat. "Buckle up, Rosebud."

She pulled the seatbelt across her chest and fastened it before grinning at him. "Silly, Daddy. I've been driving for half my life. I always wear my seatbelt. You don't have to worry about me. I can take care of myself."

He chuckled. "Is that so?"

"Yes." She sat straighter, feeling proud of herself.

He tapped the roof of her car with his hand. "I'll follow you to the bank and then home."

As she watched him climb into his SUV, she thought something was strange about the last few things he'd said. Actually, he hadn't said much at all. Mostly, he'd listened, but it had seemed like he definitely had some things he wanted to say. Did they have anything to do with the numbers he'd texted her? She hadn't had a chance to ask him what *one*, *two*, and *three* meant.

I guess I'll find out when we get home.

Chapter Ten

Adam was pretty sure his Little girl had no idea she was about to get her bottom spanked. Even though their relationship was new, he needed to make sure his little Rosebud understood that Daddy made rules for a reason, and he expected her to follow them. When she didn't, there would be consequences.

He'd spent some time today pondering his normal schedule and readjusting. If his Little girl wasn't going to get home until about nine-thirty at night, they needed to eat dinner at that hour, which meant shifting his evening schedule.

He'd already started making changes at work so he could come in later every morning and work later in the evenings. He wanted his schedule to mirror Rose's as much as possible. He would still have plenty of time to prepare dinner before she got off work.

Adam opened the garage door as they approached, hoping his Little girl would notice he'd cleared one side so her car would fit too. She pulled tentatively into the driveway, but waited for him to pass her and park.

He came to her window as soon as he hopped down from the SUV. "This will be your spot from now on, Rosebud," he said, pointing at the empty garage slot in front of her.

"Really?" She stared at it and then him.

He furrowed his brow. "Are you afraid you'll hit something, Rosebud?"

She shook her head. "No. It just feels so..."

"Like you live here?" he supplied.

She nodded. "That's it."

"More than unpacking your belongings into my drawers this morning, naughty girl?"

She flinched and met his gaze with wide eyes. Her mouth dropped open.

He pointed at the garage again. "Park, Little girl. We'll talk inside." He watched her ease her car into the spot even though there was more than enough space for her smaller vehicle.

Meeting her at her door, he opened it and helped her out before leading her into the kitchen. After shutting the garage door and the door to the house, he turned to find her staring at him, eyes still wide. "Am I in trouble?" Her lip quivered and a tear fell down her cheek.

Adam closed the distance and pulled her into his arms before tipping her chin back and kissing her briefly. "No need for tears, Rosebud. Little girls make mistakes. When they do, they get disciplined, wipe the slate, and start over."

"Is this why you were texting me numbers? Did I make three mistakes today?" Her voice was shaky.

"Yep. Do you know what any of them were?" He held her tight, wanting her to understand that he loved her dearly no matter what.

"Uhhh... Noo..." She didn't meet his gaze.

"I bet you can guess."

Her shoulders drooped. "I forgot to text you when I got out of the shower."

"Yes. That's one."

She lifted her face, her eyes lighting up. "I did eat my lunch. All of it," she blurted.

He chuckled. "I'm glad, Rosebud. That doesn't erase the naughty things though, does it?"

She shook her head.

"What did you consume that you weren't supposed to?"

She winced. "Oh, that. How did you know?"

He chuckled again. "You left your coffee mug in the bathroom on the counter."

She groaned.

"What did I say about coffee?"

"But, Daddy, I need coffee in the mornings. I don't think I can make it through the day without it."

He lifted a brow. "What did Daddy say?"

She sighed adorably. "You said to try eating real foods that are good for me to see if I have enough energy that way instead."

"And you went behind my back and defied me as soon as I left the house. Is that a very nice girl?"

"No, Sir. It's pretty high on the naughty scale. I'm sorry."

"And one more thing. You said you were almost late for work today. Why was that, Rosebud?"

She stiffened. "That wasn't my fault, Daddy. I can't make traffic disappear."

She had no idea how cute she was defending herself. "You could have left a few minutes earlier though, couldn't you?"

"I suppose, but I didn't know that."

"What you *did* know was that Daddy said he would unpack your things after work today. Instead, you spent several minutes doing so yourself, time you could have spent in the car arriving at work earlier."

"Oh. Right. I was just excited to have a couple drawers and I wanted to feel like I lived here. I didn't think it was a big deal."

"I know, Rosebud. Daddy is sharp. I understand what you were thinking, but when Daddy tells you to do something or not do it, it's for a reason. In this case, I'm trying hard to help make your life easier while you work long hours through the holiday season. One of the ways I can help take some of your load is to do things for you to ease your busy schedule."

"Things like unpack my suitcase and cook for me?"

"Exactly. I'm going to think of more things I can do to help you too because that's what Daddies do. We try to think of every detail. As the owner of my company, I have the staff that will allow me to lighten my load for a while so I can be here for you, but you have to respect Daddy's rules and obey them."

"Yes, Sir. I'm sorry. I'll be better tomorrow."

He kissed her forehead. "I know you will, Rosebud. But today you need to be disciplined."

"Are you going to spank me?" She shifted her weight back and forth before squeezing her legs together.

"I am, and then you're going to stand in timeout and think about the changes you'll make tomorrow to avoid another spanking."

"Timeout?" Her voice squeaked.

"Yep." He nodded toward the corner of the kitchen. "Right over there. It's the perfect corner for naughty Little girls who need to think about their mistakes."

"But..." She squirmed. "What about..."

He hauled her flat against him again and hugged her close. "You're going to learn that Little girls who misbehave and get their bottoms spanked do not get to follow that discipline up with orgasms."

She shuddered in his embrace. "But Daddy, the last time you spanked me..."

He kissed the top of her head. "I know. Your pussy got wet and swollen. I suspect it will happen again this time too, but you'll be standing in timeout while the arousal subsides."

When he leaned her back, he found her face flushed. "I don't think I'm going to like this plan."

"I suspect not, but you'll think twice before you blatantly defy Daddy tomorrow, won't you?"

She nodded. "Yes, Sir."

He took a step back and reached for the hem of her Stuff-It T-shirt, pulling it over her head before she could protest.

"You're going to take my clothes off too?" she hedged as he bent to remove her shoes and unbutton her jeans.

"Yep. Daddy will always want your bottom bare before I spank you."

"But we're in the kitchen..."

He smiled up at her as he tugged her jeans and panties down her legs. "We sure are. Do you think spankings only occur in certain rooms?"

"No, but..." She glanced around as she held on to his shoulders while he removed her jeans. "It's just so...open in here."

"No one is here but me, Rosebud. No one can see you but me. Daddy would never expose you to anyone else. You can count on that."

"What if someone walks through the backyard?" she asked in a very Little voice, glancing at the windows.

"I don't think the gardener will be coming at almost ten at night."

She chewed on her bottom lip. He could practically see her trying to come up with another excuse. He didn't let her think about it long, however. He rose, quickly removed her bra, and led her to a chair at the kitchen table.

Adam doubted she had any idea how gorgeous she was, all soft curves and flushed skin with the added goosebumps for good measure. Her pretty breasts were high and tight, the nipples hard points he was going to avoid entirely.

This was hard for him. His cock was stiff. He'd rather make love to her than punish her, but she needed to learn that Daddy was no pushover. So, he sat, guided her to one side of his lap, and lowered her across his thighs.

As he rubbed her cute bottom, he set one hand on the small of her back. "Keep your thighs parted, Rosebud. Daddy will spank you extra if you try to rub your clit against me or squeeze it."

She shuddered but her precious legs parted.

"Keep your hands tucked under you. If you reach back, Daddy might swat them and hurt you."

"Okay." Her voice was soft. Reverent. "I won't move them, Daddy."

"Good girl." He rubbed her bottom a few more seconds before lifting his palm and swatting her.

She flinched but didn't protest. She wasn't as stunned as she'd been the first time he'd spanked her. Eventually she would know what to expect and not stiffen over his lap. But this was new to her. For now, he needed to take things slower than he would in the future.

After warming her up enough that she was relaxed against him, he increased the pressure, spanking her harder until her bottom was a lovely shade of pink. Just dark enough to serve as a reminder but not too red that she would bruise.

When he was finished, he rubbed her heated skin again. "Such a good girl. I'm proud of you for accepting your spanking, Rosebud." He stood her on her feet, holding her by the hips to make sure she didn't sway too far.

She sniffled. "I'm sorry I was naughty, Daddy."

He kissed her forehead, stood, and took her hand to lead her to the naughty corner. "You'll stand here now while I get dinner on the table."

She inched into the corner, glancing up at him. "I don't think I like this idea, Daddy," she murmured.

"You're not supposed to like it, Rosebud. It's punishment."

She sighed as he guided her so that her forehead touched the corner, her nose almost against the wall. "Clasp your hands behind your back and part your legs, Rosebud," he encouraged.

She shivered as she obeyed him, whimpering. "Daddy..."

He set a hand on her back. "What, Little girl?"

"My, uh, my pussy is needy."

"I know, Rosebud. You enjoy having your bottom spanked. I don't think you're going to enjoy standing in timeout though.

After a few minutes, your arousal will lessen, and then we can eat."

She shivered again, a sweet sigh leaving her mouth. "Okay, Daddy," she murmured.

Adam was so proud of her he couldn't stop smiling as he headed for the oven to remove the casserole he'd made earlier in the evening. He'd turned the oven down to its lowest setting to keep it warm while he'd gone to meet Rose after work.

He was glad he'd chosen a comfort food now because his Little girl was going to need it after her punishment. After putting the casserole on the table, adding a tossed salad and place settings, he returned to Rose.

"Do you feel better, Little Rosebud?"

She sniffled and nodded. "Yes, Daddy. Thank you for disciplining me. I'll be a good girl tomorrow."

He cupped her face and kissed her forehead. "Let's wipe away those tears and eat some dinner." He led her to the sink, wet a washcloth, and gently cleaned away her tears and most of her makeup.

As he guided her to the table, she glanced at him. "I can't eat naked, Daddy."

He chuckled. "Are you sure? I don't think it would be a hardship for me," he teased.

She shook her head. "Can I at least have a shirt?"

He reached over his head, pulled off the T-shirt he'd changed into after work, and turned to put it on her.

She giggled. "Daddy..."

"What?" He pulled out her chair and helped her sit before pushing her in.

"This isn't better," she stated.

"Why not? You're covered."

She smiled broadly as her gaze roamed his chest. "But now you're not. And I don't know if I can eat with your sexy chest exposed."

He laughed. "I bet you can find a way." He dished up a helping of casserole onto her plate.

She leaned over it and inhaled deeply. "That smells so good. It's ooey gooey and cheesy!"

"Yep. I thought you would like it."

"I'm sure I will." She kicked her feet but then winced.

He glanced at her, fighting a grin. "Does your bottom hurt?"

"Uh huh."

He dished up some salad too, giving her a reasonably sized portion. "Eat your dinner, Rosebud."

She took a bite and moaned around it. "That's so good, Daddy. Delish!"

"I'm glad you like it. Drink your milk too. You need the calcium. I noticed you didn't drink much this morning. You traded it for coffee."

She winced. "I'm sorry, Daddy. I'll try your way tomorrow, but what if it doesn't work and I'm a raving bitch by eleven in the morning?"

He shot her a narrowed gaze. "Language, Little girl."

"Sorry, Daddy, but it's true. I might be that B word if I don't have coffee."

"If you feel that out of sorts, we'll revisit the subject and wean you off gradually instead. How does that sound?"

Her face lit up. "That might work."

"Try it. Stick with water, fruit juices, and milk for three days. I bet you'll feel more alert and energetic. If not, we'll renegotiate."

"Okay. That's fair." She put another bite of casserole in her mouth, moaned around it, and swallowed. "You're the bestest Daddy ever."

He considered pinching himself to be sure he wasn't dreaming. Somehow in less than a week, he'd met his forever Little girl and essentially moved her into his house.

She was precious beyond words, even when she was

naughty. He suspected she would continue to make mistakes for a while as she learned that Daddy meant business and began to trust his decisions and obey his rules, but the structure would be good for her.

She looked so cute sitting in his kitchen, wearing nothing but his T-shirt, squirming around because her bottom was sore. When she picked up the sippy cup and took a long drink, he melted a bit more. She was so perfect for him.

Everything was going too well. Was he overlooking anything? It was hard to imagine anything could possibly happen to disrupt the path that had guided him to his Little girl.

Chapter Eleven

Things got busier and busier over the next few days. Work got more hectic as the holiday approached. Every day there were more customers than the day before. Rose began to worry she didn't have enough staff to get through the season, but she was also afraid if she added another person, there wouldn't be enough work to keep them after the holidays were over.

Her Daddy was amazing. He was her rock. Her life wouldn't be running nearly as smoothly as it was without him. He was there for her when she got up in the mornings and there to tuck her into his bed late at night.

Adam cooked and cleaned. He made sure she ate properly, feeding her breakfast and dinner under his supervision and sending her to work with a lunch that would sustain her throughout the day.

She didn't even think about skipping lunch anymore because she was always excited to see what he'd packed. He was an amazing cook. His lunches made the other employees jealous when they found her eating in the breakroom.

The first two days without caffeine left her with a slight headache and the jitters, but by the third day, she felt much better. Once again, Daddy knew best. She had tried to follow his guidance every day, and she hadn't ended up standing in the corner with a sore bottom since the night she'd had three infractions in one day.

On her fourth morning sleeping with Daddy, her phone rang so early Daddy's alarm hadn't gone off yet. She recognized the sound, but she was groggy enough that she couldn't quite manage to pull herself to sitting before Daddy reached across her and snagged it from the nightstand.

"We better answer it, Rosebud. At this hour, it might be important."

She pushed to sitting while he swiped his finger across the screen before the call would be missed. He pushed the speaker button and held it out.

"Hello?" she said. Her voice was so scratchy, she had to clear it and try again. "Hello?"

"Rose? This is Johnny, the night watchman from the mall."

"Oh, hi, Johnny." She sat up straighter. "Is something wrong?"

"You could say that. There was a water main break in your wing of the mall overnight. There's no damage to your store, but we had to shut off electricity to that wing. The water department is on their way out. I can't be sure how long it will take to fix it, but you won't be able to open Stuff-It today."

"Oh." She was waking up by degrees, but still processing his information. "Thank you for letting me know. I'll call my employees."

"Good. Someone will contact you when we know how long it's going to take to make the repairs. Enjoy your accidental vacation day." He ended the call.

Rose sighed. "I guess I should consider it a gift, but it's hard when I think about all the holiday revenue we'll miss out on."

Daddy rubbed her back. "I bet they'll have you back up and running in a day or two. Like you said, let's call it a gift. I'll cancel my meetings for today, and we'll both play hooky from life." He grinned.

She couldn't help but join his enthusiasm. "You know what I'd really like to do?"

"What's that, Rosebud?"

"I'd like it if you took me to your plant. I haven't had a chance to see where you work. I want to know how gumballs are made."

He tugged her back under the covers. "That's a great idea, Rosebud, but first I want to take advantage of other bonuses we get as a result of this forced vacation day."

She giggled, but her body came alive fast as soon as her Daddy lowered his face to her breast, cupping it as he circled her nipple with his tongue.

Suddenly, she felt very grateful for the day off.

Adam ushered Rose into the main door of the gumball factory. There was a small reception area for visitors to purchase products. A woman at the front desk smiled and stood to greet them.

"Mr. Connell. I wasn't expecting you."

"Hi, Alice. I'd like you to meet someone very special to me. This is Rose Stewart."

"Hi, Ms. Stewart. Welcome to gumball heaven," the pleasant young woman said. Her dancing eyes made her words even more humorous.

"Gumball heaven? I love it. Hi, Alice." Rose looked up at Adam as she realized how smart he was to have such a fun receptionist.

"I'm going to give Rose the grand expedition around the factory, Alice. Don't tell anyone I'm here. They'll try to rope me into doing something other than playing tour guide."

"You've got it, boss." She made a sign of locking her lips closed and throwing away the key.

"Thanks, Alice," Adam said with a laugh before urging Rose on with a guiding hand at the small of her back. "Let's get started. Goggles and hardhats first."

By the time Rose had donned the protective equipment, she was so excited she bounced on her toes. "Can we go inside the plant now?"

"Picture first. I want to remember this. Get close," Adam instructed, holding his phone out to take a selfie. He took several.

"Can we make funny faces in one?" Rose pleaded.

"Let's try it!" Adam encouraged her and took several photos of their silliness. When he flipped through all the pictures, Rose's heart melted. The poses made her feel like they were truly a couple.

"I'll send them to you," Adam said as he tapped his screen.

Rose's phone buzzed in her pocket. "Thank you!"

"Ready to dive into the gumball world?" he asked, guiding her toward the big, heavy door leading into the factory.

"Please!"

Adam escorted Rose from one station to the next. She watched the skilled employees load the gum base into the mixers with flavoring. Today, they were making a batch of cinnamon gum. The smell was amazing, but strong.

As that combined, they followed another cart to the extruder. It shaped the mixture into hollow tubes that then got chopped and shaped into balls. Rose was almost dizzy watching all the machinery work so quickly to create them. Those circular treats then went to huge tumblers that almost looked like clothes dryers. There the coloring was added several times to coat the balls as they rolled around inside.

The final stop was the packaging. Some were individually wrapped while others were dumped into larger plastic containers. Adam plucked one from the conveyer belt with a gloved hand and handed it to her.

Immediately, Rose popped it into her mouth and chewed. The flavor exploded in her mouth. That one was bubble gum flavored.

"Yum! It tastes different than I'm used to," she said cautiously. "Maybe fresher?"

"You can't get any fresher than that one." Adam laughed before adding, "The assortments in the gift shop are just as fresh. Would you like to take some cinnamon gumballs home with us?"

"I'd love that. Do you give tours a lot?"

"We used to have groups of school kids come through. Unfortunately, all the safety precautions make that impossible to do now. It's a shame. Everyone can watch the process online, but it's not the same as being here."

"And smelling everything. It's so much fun," Rose gushed.

"I'm glad you enjoyed seeing the factory. Let's head to the gift store, pick up some treats for you, and head out for lunch. All this activity has made me ravenous." He wiggled his eyebrows to express that he was not speaking solely about the factory excursion.

"Daddy!" she whispered furiously as she looked around to see if anyone was listening. Thankfully, all the employees worked at a distance from them. As she scanned the factory, a man began to wave in their direction.

"That man seems to be signaling you," Rose suggested, pointing his way.

"That's the foreman. Let me go check with him. Why don't you go through that door and take off your protective gear? If you remember the way, you could go check out the choices in the gift shop," he suggested after acknowledging the man's signal with a wave of his hand. "I won't be too long."

"Don't rush. I'll be fine," she assured him.

At the door, Rose paused to watch him walk away. The

view was extraordinary. Realizing where she was, Rose hurried through the doorway and stowed her glasses in her hard hat on the table. Confident she knew where she was going, she headed down the hallway and turned the corner. *Whoops! That area doesn't look familiar.*

As she turned around to try another route, Rose spotted a bathroom and decided to duck inside. Choosing a stall from the line available, she quickly availed herself of the facilities. She had just finished and was righting her clothes when someone else entered the bathroom.

"I thought today was going to be a total waste when Mr. Hotbuns wasn't here," a female voice observed.

Rose realized more than one person had entered. She tipped her head down and saw three sets of feet.

"He was supposed to be out today. I was totally bummed," another voice shared. "Then he came strutting down the line with the foreman. I think every female employee and a few of the males all swooned."

"You two are awful, talking about the boss like that," the third voice criticized.

"Miss High and Mighty, didn't I see you running over there to talk to him?" the second voice asked.

"That's business. He asked me to let him know how the new extruder was working."

"You didn't go talk to him while he was showing that woman around. They looked pretty friendly," the first voice pointed out.

Hearing three stall doors close, Rose flushed her toilet quickly and rushed out without washing her hands. She'd do that later. Right now, she wanted to avoid running into the women who'd ogled her Daddy.

Rushing back the other way, Rose burst into the welcoming area, visibly startling Alice. "Oops! Sorry. That door opened faster than I expected." She wandered casually over to the hand sanitizer dispenser at the side of the room and took care of her hands.

"Did you want to pick up a few treats?" Alice said, smiling as she stood up from her chair.

"Definitely. I loved the cinnamon scent. Do you have any of those?" Rose asked.

"They just brought a fresh batch in. There are some yummy fruit flavors, too. They're my favorite. If you like to blow bubbles, the traditional bubble gum balls are what you want," Alice advised.

"Who doesn't like to blow bubbles?"

"Right? Let's get you an assortment."

Within minutes, Alice had a large tote bag filled with a huge assortment. "That should keep you busy for a couple of weeks," the receptionist announced.

"Weeks? It will take months to chew all that!" Rose exclaimed as she pulled her phone wallet from her pocket to pay.

"Put that away. This batch is on Mr. Connell. He'll flay me alive if I let you give me any money."

"Thank you. Is he this sweet to everyone?" Rose asked.

"He's a very polite man but I never forget that Mr. Connell is a shrewd businessman as well. The factory wasn't doing too well when he took over. He's made a ton of improvements in the last couple of years. I was working on the line back then. I saw everything first hand."

"Does he date his employees?" Rose blurted.

"Mr. Connell? Not that I know of. There's plenty that flirt with him. I don't think he notices. I've always suspected he was searching for someone special. I'm glad he's found you," Alice shared.

"I'm glad I found her, too," Adam's deep voice commented from the doorway.

"Sorry, Mr. Connell. I wasn't gossiping," Alice assured him quickly.

"Rose has a very inquisitive mind. I have no doubt she asked you some questions. She's used to hanging out with the creatures at Stuff-It. There are no secrets there," Adam observed, walking to Rose and hugging her to his side.

"Stuff-It? I always want to go in there, but I'm too old to make a stuffie for myself," Alice deplored.

"No one is too old for stuffies. You totally should. It's so much fun," Rose encouraged her.

"Maybe I will. Thanks. I haven't done anything just for the joy of it for a while. It could be my Christmas present to myself," Alice suggested.

Adam nodded his agreement. "I think that's a perfect idea. Now, we need to get something to eat. All the emergencies are settled. Did you get enough gumballs? This sack feels light," he observed, lifting the colorful tote bag.

"I didn't pay for it," Rose said quickly.

"Good. Thank you, Alice, for taking care of Rose while I was busy."

"Have a good day, Mr. Connell. I'll see you tomorrow," Alice answered and scurried to her desk as the phone rang.

"Let's go, Rosebud. What flavor did you get the most of?" he asked, steering her through the door.

"Guess!"

"Let's see. You practically wiggled into the mixer when they added the cinnamon flavoring. I bet that's the one you wanted over the others."

"You know me so well," she whispered as they reached the car.

When he helped her into her seat, Adam leaned close to kiss her lightly. "I'm learning all I can about my special Little girl."

Overcome with a depth of emotion she didn't expect to feel so quickly, Rose tugged his lips back to hers and kissed him passionately before settling against the seat to pull her seatbelt on.

Adam brushed her hands away and snapped it securely for

her. "Food and then back home, Rosebud. I need to get you alone."

"Yes, Daddy," she replied obediently. "Can we get a cupcake before we go home?"

"Of course. Let's go to Nibbles & Bites for lunch and then pick up some treats to have at home. What flavor do you want?"

"Santa's Kiss, of course. It's yummy."

Chapter Twelve

"Hi, Rose! I bet you're back here for Santa's Kiss cupcakes," Ellie enthused when they walked through the doors.

"We'll take a dozen. Give us a variety though. Surprises are fun too. Maybe Rose will take time for lunch if a cupcake is waiting for her dessert," Adam suggested with a meaningful look at Rose.

"We're always busy in the afternoon. Time just gets away from me," Rose explained.

Adam narrowed his gaze at her, but he was smiling.

Rose shifted her attention to the Little Cakes employees who were all sitting in a semi-circle around Ellie. She waved a hand their direction. "You've got something going on. We can come back later."

Immediately, Ellie shook her head and assured the couple, "No worries. Come meet everyone. You might know most of them, but I'll introduce you in case you don't know all of their names. These are my employee friends and my favorite people who work other places in town," Ellie shared.

"Hi, everyone," Rose said with a smile.

"I'm glad to hear you're having such success. I know how

hard it is to start a thriving business. Guess what? This is the posse I told you about that I'd like to bring to Stuff-It." Ellie paused to lean a bit closer and said, "They're Littles, too."

"How fun! I'm looking forward to seeing you all." Rose smiled at their grinning faces.

"Hi, I'm Riley. I work here at Little Cakes," a beautifully tattooed woman informed her.

A cheerful blonde spoke next. "I'm Daisy. I hope I'll get to come with the crowd, but it depends on the day. I own the floral shop just over there." She gestured toward the window.

"I'm Lark, Ellie's oldest friend from grade school."

"I've seen your picture on real estate signs," Rose exclaimed.

"That's me. Well, me with a lot of makeup, hairspray, and a good photographer," Lark pointed out.

"I recognize you," Rose said, looking at the next woman. "You've been to Stuff-It."

"Wow, you have a good memory. I'm Tori."

"I work here, too. I'm Sue. I'll go grab cupcakes for you."

"Thanks, Sue," Rose responded to the cheerful brunette as she moved behind the counter.

"We're having trouble finding a time for the group to come visit Stuff-It together," Ellie said.

"If you want to try to do a private party on a Sunday morning still, let me know and I'll work it out. But I'd love to see you any time. Beware, it's super busy right now with the holidays fast approaching. We were closed today due to a water leak in my side of the mall," Rose explained.

"Did you have any damage?" Ellie asked with a concerned expression.

"None, thank goodness," Rose answered.

"Yay!" the group cheered.

"I'll go pay for the cupcakes, Little girl, and then we're headed home for your nap," Adam announced.

Rose felt her face heat as he addressed her as a Little.

Looking around the assembled group, she saw no negative expressions on their faces. Everyone just nodded to agree with his decision.

Taking a chance, she asked, "Are you really *all* Little?"

"Yep," Riley answered for the group. "We've been lucky like you to find our Daddies. They all make us nap and take care of us. That's what Daddies do."

Adam's return kept Rose from having to respond. She smiled and waved as her Daddy escorted her out of the bakery.

"We'll come see you!" Ellie called before the door closed.

Looking over her shoulder through the large window, Rose saw everyone wave goodbye. "I liked them," she told her Daddy.

"Me, too. Now, home and nap."

"But I'm not tired," Rose protested, smothering a yawn.

"Don't lie to Daddy," he scolded her.

"Sorry."

Rose was quiet for a few minutes before adding, "Maybe a short nap?"

"That's my good Little girl," he praised.

Walking into Stuff-It the next day, Rose celebrated that everything seemed to be okay in her store. She'd tried not to worry but the concern had lingered in her mind as she enjoyed her free time with her Daddy. Expecting to be overwhelmed with business, she set up the cash register and restocked everything so they wouldn't have to scramble for supplies.

The back door closed with a slam, scaring her. No one was supposed to be here for another hour. She rushed to the door leading into the back section of the store and laughed.

"Larisa! You frightened me. What are you doing here so early?"

"Hi, boss. I knew you'd be here and need some help getting

things ready for the day. Is it okay for me to clock in early?" the dedicated employee asked.

"Definitely. Thanks for coming in!"

Rose headed back into the shop to continue her preparations. After a few minutes, Larisa joined her and made a few alterations to the window display. "I posted on social media that the gold tiger was the stuffie of the day. I added some fun facts about tigers and included a picture of an empty body waiting to be filled and taken home."

"That's not usually the bestseller for the holidays," Rose pointed out. "We have a ton of them in the back."

"I know. That's why I chose that one. We'll see if it boosts the sales. If so, we'll know the promos are helping."

"Go, you! Thanks for trying something new. Fingers crossed that it works," Rose encouraged.

By opening time, the bins were overflowing with stuffies-to-be carefully positioned to be able to make eye contact with everyone walking by. A line of people had formed at the door, and they streamed inside as Rose unlocked the door. Of course, there were a few curious shoppers who stopped to see what the bustle was all about. They too got swept up in the fun of making a new friend. Larisa and Rose were swamped.

"Put me to work," a familiar voice suggested, and Rose turned to see Alice at her side.

"Alice, you came to make a stuffie."

"I did, but I can wait. Looks like you're swamped. How can I help most?" Alice asked with a smile.

"I can't ask you to work. It must be your day off." Rose talked and rang up customers at the same time.

"Of course you can. I'm here and I'm willing."

"I'd be happy to show her the ropes," Larisa chimed in. She extended a hand. "I'm Larisa."

"That would be wonderful," Rose answered gratefully. She watched the gracious young woman jump in immediately to help. Glancing up frequently to make sure Alice was okay, Rose couldn't believe how quick she learned the process. What an amazing stroke of luck that she had come in today!

An hour later, a male voice greeted her from the side of the cash register. "Hi. I'm Alice's brother. She said you need help. I'm looking for a job. Let me lend you a hand with this line and we'll talk when you can breathe."

"What's your name?" Rose asked as she nodded her agreement.

"Deke. I've worked a cash register before. I'll watch you and then I can open that one if you want." He pointed to the second cash register that Rose hadn't ever used. There hadn't been enough business to warrant filling the till.

"Perfect!"

In ten minutes, she pulled out the excess cash and over-flowing charge slips out of the first register and rushed to the office to stash it in the bank envelope before loading the second till. Rose paused for a few seconds to text Amber to come in early if she could before dashing back into the shop. As she slid the till into the register, Rose loved seeing that Deke had every-thing under control and was chatting pleasantly with the customers as he admired the new friends they had created. *He's so hired!* Taking the next person in line, Rose worked next to him to diminish the crowd.

An hour later, they could all breathe again. The rush of shoppers didn't slow down, to her delight, but the four of them were able to handle the traffic inside the store. Amber arrived and relieved Alice who immediately searched through the bins for the stuffie she wanted to create.

"This one's on the house," Rose announced when Alice brought the soft pink teddy bear bedecked in a rainbow-colored dress, sparkly silver shoes, and a matching tiara to the cash register.

"Oh, no. I'll pay for Cinderbeara," Alice announced.

"No way. I owe you at least one stuffie for helping out and for calling Deke," Rose corrected her.

"He's super excited to be here. Deke jumped at the chance. He's considered applying here several times but didn't think the owner would want a big, burly guy working in a stuffie store," Alice explained.

"This store owner is glad to have him here. I'm definitely going to have to order some larger shirts for him to wear," Rose shared with a laugh.

"Oo, you're going to be busy again," Alice pointed out as a group walked in together.

"Those are my friends. They're here to have fun. I'll just put them to work as well if I need to. Thank you again, Alice. I hope I see you again," Rose said quickly as the group approached.

"I bet we'll run into each other somewhere," Alice suggested with a wink.

Rose didn't have time to wonder what she alluded to as Lark led the crew of Littles into the store.

Rose was surprised to see several of the group of friends from Little Cakes. Ellie, Daisy, Lark, and Riley. She clapped her hands as she greeted them. "I can't believe you're here. How did you all manage to get off work in the middle of the day?"

Ellie gave Rose a hug as they all gathered around her. "We realized there was no way we could all be off at the same time. Not even on a Sunday morning. Plus, Sunday mornings are your only free time. We didn't want to drag you out of bed on your only day to sleep in, so here we are!"

"But don't you need to be at Little Cakes?"

"This is the best time of day for us to escape. It's after the lunch rush and before kids get out of school. Sue and Tori stayed behind to make sure any customers are taken care of," Ellie informed her.

Riley giggled. "They were jealous though. We'll have to swap with them so they can come to Stuff-It soon while Ellie and I stay behind."

Lark hugged Rose next. "I don't happen to have any houses to show this afternoon."

Daisy was last to greet Rose with yet another hug. "I have extra help in Blooms by Daisy for this month too, so I snuck away."

"Need any help, boss?" At the deep voice, Rose spun around to face the man she hoped would become her newest employee, Deke. She hadn't had a chance yet to formally hire him, but she would speak to him as soon as there was a longer lull.

"I'm good, Deke. Thanks. These are my friends."

The burly man stroked his beard and smiled. He was certainly a big guy, but already Rose could tell he was a softy inside. She wondered if he was a Daddy.

"Ah, good. Nice to meet you all," Deke said. "I'd ask your names, but we're so busy I'm certain I would forget all of them in seconds. I'll go help the couple heading our way with the toddler. Let me know if any of you need anything."

Rose smiled as Deke greeted the elderly couple who appeared to be shopping with their grandchild.

"Wow, Deke seems nice. How long has he worked here?" Ellie asked.

"He just started this morning. He caught on fast," Rose informed her. She turned toward the Stuff-It bins. "Let's pick out new friends!"

It didn't take long for all four women to pick out a stuffie and start the process. It was fun listening to each of them as they tried out different names and laughed as they discarded some outlandish ones.

An hour later, they had all finished and were ready to head back to their respective jobs, new stuffies in hand.

Ellie gave Rose another hug as they said their goodbyes. "I know you haven't lived here long and you're super busy with Stuff-It, but I hope you'll be able to come to Blaze one night soon with your Daddy. We have so much fun in the daycare. I know Adam is a member."

Rose nodded. "He's mentioned Blaze. It sounds like fun. I'm so glad I met all of you. As soon as I can get away for an evening, I'll ask him to take me."

Lark bounced excitedly. "We love new friends."

Rose couldn't stop grinning as she watched the four women skip away down the mall. She'd known Ellie and Riley at least peripherally from many trips to Little Cakes, but she could tell in time all of them would be a great addition to her growing list of friends.

"Your phone's ringing, boss," Larisa called out from behind the cash registers as she returned from the back room.

"Oops." Rose glanced around, determined everything was under control, and rushed back to her office. She winced as she picked up her phone. Four missed texts from Adam. Two calls.

She decided to call him, and she chewed on her bottom lip as she waited for him to answer.

Luckily he picked up on the second ring. "Hey, Rosebud. Have you been busy today?"

"Yes, Daddy." She glanced at the door to her office, but no one could hear her. "Swamped. Did you know Alice came in this morning?"

"Did she? She mentioned wanting to go sometime. I guess she chose today since she had the morning off. Did she find a new friend?"

Rose nodded excitedly even though her Daddy couldn't see her. "She did much more than that. She was a godsend. I was swamped. She jumped in and started working."

Daddy chuckled. "That sounds like Alice. She's a hard worker."

"Even more than that, she called her brother to come help."

"Deke? He's a great guy. That was kind of her."

"It was. Apparently, he's looking for a job. He's been here working most of the day. I haven't even had a chance to sit down with him and ask him if he'd like to start working here."

"Oh, that would be amazing, but he's a bit overqualified. I'm not sure he'll take you up on that offer. He just moved here to be closer to Alice, but he was a department store manager before he moved to town."

"Really? Oh, my. You're right. He's not going to want to work in a silly little stuffie store." Rose sighed. Darn.

"Now, let's not get too hasty. I have some thoughts about that."

"Really?" Rose couldn't imagine what might lure Deke into working for her. She couldn't possibly pay him what he was worth.

"For one thing, since he doesn't have a job yet, I bet he could at least get you through the holidays, and I know him well enough to be certain he's a trustworthy employee. Maybe this is the perfect temporary solution to your problem," Daddy suggested.

"What problem is that?" Rose frowned and stiffened.

"You need some help, Rosebud," he said gently. "You're burning your candle at both ends."

Rose took a deep breath, not responding. He might be right, but this was her business. Her baby. Her life. She'd put several months of blood, sweat, and tears into making Stuff-It get off the ground. She didn't like his implication.

"Rose... Are you still there, Little girl?"

She flinched. "Yes, but I need to go. It's a busy day. I'll talk to you tonight." She ended the call without waiting for a response. She didn't jump up to run back out front though. Instead she sat at her desk, thinking.

This was the first time she'd felt aggravated with her Daddy. She knew he meant well, but she didn't want him to interfere with her business. She was capable of deciding if she was working too hard. She didn't need him telling her what to do.

She glanced at the small fridge she kept in her office. She

hadn't had lunch yet. Without a doubt, she should take this opportunity to eat whatever Adam had packed for her this morning, but she felt stubborn and frustrated, so she ignored her growling stomach, put her aggravation out of her mind, and headed back to the front. She had a business to run. Customers to help.

Chapter Thirteen

Adam was confused and worried as he stared at his phone. Had his Little girl just hung up on him? Why on earth would she do such a thing? He couldn't imagine what he'd said to upset her.

Maybe I'm overreacting and she's simply busy.

Adam headed to a meeting, but he struggled to listen to the presentation one of his senior employees was giving about the amount of money they would be saving as soon as the new packaging line was in place.

He glanced at his watch several times. The day was dragging. He checked his phone over and over. No messages from Rose. It wasn't sitting well with him, so he eventually gave up trying to focus, made his excuses, and left the factory. He needed to see his Little girl, look her in the eyes, reassure himself she wasn't angry with him.

Fifteen minutes later, he was rushing through the mall with such long strides he had to force himself to slow down before he knocked into someone. By the time he reached Stuff-It, he was in a panic.

There were three groups of customers in the store. A quick scan of the room told him Larisa was helping one, Amber another, and Deke the last. Where was Rose?

Deke glanced up from where he was assisting someone at the checkout and beamed. "Hey, Adam. Rose didn't mention you were coming by this afternoon. I think she's in her office."

Adam struggled to smile and nod as he rushed past Alice's brother. "Thank you," he muttered. Seconds later, he found his Little girl pacing back and forth in her small office. She didn't notice him as he approached. She looked fit to kill though. Her hands were fisted. It looked like she'd been running her fingers through her hair because the cute bear clip she often wore on top was askew. She was also muttering to herself.

"Rosebud?"

She jerked to a stop, spun in his direction, and froze. Her eyes widened. "What are you doing here?"

He frowned. "I didn't like how our earlier conversation ended. I was worried you were mad at me. I couldn't focus at work, so I gave up trying and came here." He stepped inside, closed the door, and inched toward her.

"I *am* mad at you," she informed him. She stood taller, but she was so much shorter than him that even pumping her chest out and rising to her full height didn't help much. He recognized an angry Little girl when he saw one though.

Forcing himself to be calm, he took a deep breath and stopped approaching. "I see. What did I do, Rosebud?" Inside he was in a panic, but he tried not to let it show outwardly.

She threw her hands up in the air, obviously exasperated. "You can't just interfere with my business, Adam. This is my job. It's important to me. I don't need you thinking you can take over or control things that pertain to my business."

He tried to think back on what he'd said that had gotten her so flustered and upset. They'd been discussing Deke at the time. "I'm sorry, Rosebud, but please tell me specifically what I said." He kept his voice calm.

She spun around to walk behind her desk, putting more space between them.

Adam palmed the back of the chair across from her, pulled

it out a few inches, and lowered himself onto it. Maybe if he wasn't standing so tall and imposing, she wouldn't feel as intimidated. He didn't like his Little girl feeling overwhelmed by him.

Rose dropped into her desk chair and rubbed her temples. She was trembling and looked on the verge of tears.

"Rose..." A knot formed in his throat. He hated seeing her like this. He wanted to round the desk, scoop her up, and cradle her in his arms, rocking her until she calmed.

"Can we talk about this later? I'm too emotional right now, and I don't want to cry at work," she suggested.

Adam considered her request for a moment and then shook his head. "No, Rosebud. I don't think that's a good idea. It was obvious when I arrived that you weren't getting anything productive done anyway. I think you need to get everything off your chest right now so I can help you work it out and the rest of your day can be productive."

She glared at him. "You can't Daddy me at work, Adam. You can't boss me around and tell me what to do."

This was bad. Worse than he'd expected. But he wasn't going to back down. He set his elbows on his knees and leaned forward. "Little girl, I wouldn't be a very good Daddy if I left you here angry and near tears. I won't do that. I'm your Daddy all the time, even when things are tough, even when you think you don't want me to be, even when you're mad at me."

Her lip was quivering. Her eyes were watery too. The dam was about to break, and he thought it might be for the best. None of her employees out front needed to know. The door was closed.

When she didn't continue arguing, Adam stood, returned to the door, and locked it. Next, he rounded the desk, lifted his Little girl off her chair, and took her spot, settling her on his lap.

He was grateful she didn't fight him. Small blessings. She curled up and covered her face. "Maybe I'm just tired and I overreacted. I don't know."

"I know you're exhausted, Rosebud." He rubbed her back.

"You work very long hours. Even the forced vacation day wasn't enough to make up for the stress of your job. That's why I suggested Deke..." *Ohhh.*

It suddenly dawned on him what this was all about. Deke. He'd suggested she needed more help.

She stiffened once again and leaned back, scowling. "I can take care of my store without help," she insisted.

Adam gently removed the crooked bear clip from the top of her head and smoothed her hair back. "I know you can, Rosebud. You can do anything in the world you put your mind to, but at what expense? You've been working twelve hours a day for months. Business is going well. I know it's still new and scary, but I bet if you take a close look at your books, you'd find you can afford some help." He hoped he was right. Based on the number of customers he knew went through this store every day he was confident in his assessment without seeing the numbers.

"You think I should hire Deke to manage the store." Her lip continued to quiver. "You think I can't do it without him."

Ahh. Adam shook his head. "That's not true. I know for a fact you can do it alone. You've been doing it alone for months. You can continue to do so, but aren't you tired, Rosebud? Wouldn't it be nice to sleep in some days? Go on a vacation? Read more than one or two pages in a book before you fall asleep?"

She stared at him but at least she didn't interrupt, and she wasn't as defensive.

"I would never suggest you can't do something, Rosebud. Never ever. You're multitalented and perfectly capable. But you're also my Little girl, and my job as your Daddy is to take care of you and make suggestions that might help improve your quality of life. That's what Daddies do."

She sighed.

Good sign, so he continued, "When you told me Deke was here, ideas formed quickly in my head. Deke is a hard worker.

He knows about sales. He's held a managerial position for many years. I have no idea if he has any interest in stuffies or not. I haven't asked him, but it's worth looking into. If you hired a manager, you would still be the owner. You would still get final say on everything that happens in Stuff-It, but a huge weight would be lifted off your shoulders, and you wouldn't have to worry all the time."

She lowered her gaze and leaned into him, setting her head on his shoulder.

Adam rubbed her back, feeling the tension ease with every passing minute. He kissed the top of her head. "I love you, Rosebud. My heart seized when I realized I'd done something to make you so very unhappy."

"I'm sorry, Daddy," she finally murmured.

He leaned her back and met her gaze. "I'm sorry, too. I blundered through my suggestion. I'll try to do better next time and maybe if I make a suggestion in the future, you could take a deep breath and talk it out with me. My ideas might work for you or not. I know you won't choose to take my business advice every time, and that's okay. But..." He lifted her hand and kissed her knuckles before stroking her shaking fingers.

Adam suspected part of the reason she was so upset and frustrated had to do with a certain lunch he would bet his last dollar was still sitting in her fridge. "But," he continued, "everything else that's not related to your store falls under my jurisdiction. As your Daddy, I expect you to obey my rules. Did you eat your lunch today?"

She slowly shook her head.

"I didn't think so. Do you think perhaps part of the reason you're so upset is because you didn't get enough nourishment in your body today?"

She slowly nodded. "Maybe."

"Little girls who don't eat get hangry, don't they?"

"Yes, Sir," she mumbled.

"How about you go grab your lunch from the fridge and sit

and eat it while we talk some more," he suggested with a pat on her bottom.

"Okay, Daddy." She slid off his lap and shuffled toward the fridge. When she returned, holding the teddy bear lunchbox he'd sent with her to work, he set it on the desk, lifted her onto his lap, and snuggled her against him.

"What's in it, Daddy? You always make such yummy lunches. Part of why I didn't open it was because I was mad at you and I knew it would make me smile and ruin my mad," she admitted.

He chuckled as he opened the lunchbox for her. "I'm glad my food makes you happy, Rosebud."

She drew in a breath. "That looks so good." As soon as he held it up, she snatched the thick sandwich from his hands and took a huge bite. "Mmm." After swallowing, she asked, "What's in it today, Daddy?"

"Turkey, avocado, sprouts, lettuce, tomatoes, provolone, and wholegrain bread." He gave her a squeeze, relieved she was no longer shooting daggers at him.

"So good." She devoured it, moaning around every bite in a way that made Adam grit his teeth to keep his cock from reacting. He was failing, especially when she squirmed her little bottom on his lap.

As soon as she ate the last bite, she reached for the cupcake. He'd put it in a closed container, preventing her from seeing which type it was. He did this every day so her desserts were always a surprise.

She giggled as soon as she opened it. "Santa's Kiss! I love this kind." She twisted in his arms and hugged him tight. "Thank you, Daddy. Thank you for coming over here and fixing things so I wouldn't be mad anymore. I'm sorry I was naughty and hung up on you and didn't listen to you. I won't do it again. I promise."

He held her close, nuzzling her neck, breathing in her scent. "Couples fight sometimes, Rosebud. It will happen. But I want you to talk things out with me so we never go very long angry at each other, okay?"

"Yes, Daddy."

"And when we get home, I'm going to spank your bottom for not eating your lunch. I bet some of your frustration could have been avoided if you'd eaten properly." He lifted a brow.

She sighed. "You're right, Daddy. I won't complain when it's time for my spanking."

"Good girl. Now, how about if you finish that cupcake and get back out on the floor. Daddy needs to get back to work. If Deke is still here when you lock up, have him walk you to your car. If not, call me to come meet you. I bet you have a lot more money than usual in the store today. I don't want you carrying it out to your car alone."

"Yes, Daddy. I will. I promise."

Chapter Fourteen

The rest of the day went by smoothly and fast. Rose felt much better after she'd eaten and talked to her Daddy. Plus, she realized he was probably right. From the moment Deke had arrived to save the day, the atmosphere in the store had improved.

Rose watched him closely. He was efficient and knew how to run a store. He might not know much about stuffies, but he learned fast and was always one step ahead of anything that was running low or needed attention.

By the time they closed the gate to end the day, Rose was mentally calculating just how much she could afford to pay him and praying he would be willing to consider becoming the manager.

The thought of spending more time with her Daddy was so appealing that it no longer mattered to her if she had to part with some of her income to do so. It would be worth every dime.

Before she'd met Adam, she'd been in a constant frenzy worrying about finances and ensuring her business was viable. She refused to consider failure. But Stuff-It was a thriving store. With Larisa's help with social media and Amber coming in after school, they'd been doing amazingly. Adding a manager though... That would be heaven.

She really wished she hadn't been so quick to anger earlier at her Daddy's suggestion.

Deke smiled at her as he locked the gate. "I had a great time here today, Rose."

"Thank you so much for helping me out. You're amazing."

He shrugged his huge shoulders. "It was my pleasure. I've only been in town a few weeks. I haven't yet decided what sort of job I want to do next. Any chance you're in the market for a manager?"

Rose beamed. "Now that you mention it... I hadn't considered hiring a manager until today, but your presence has made me think. Maybe it wouldn't be a bad idea. I talked to Adam when he was here earlier. He thinks you'd be an excellent addition to my team. I'll need to crunch some numbers first and see what I can afford. Can you come in tomorrow? We'll talk then."

Deke held out a hand. "Sounds like a plan. I know I won't make as much money as I was making in the big city, but the cost of living is significantly less in this town too, so I bet we can come up with something we can agree on."

Rose shook his hand, feeling far lighter than she had all day, or perhaps in weeks.

"Need me to do anything else for you tonight?"

"Nope. You've been so much help. Go on home. I'll just finish up some bookwork and be out of here in a few minutes."

Deke narrowed his gaze. "You have someone to walk you out, right?"

"Yep."

Deke dug into his pocket and produced a business card, which he handed to Rose. "In case you need to get ahold of me, Rose. It was a pleasure. I don't remember when I've had this much fun at work. The day flew by. Seeing the faces of everyone as they go through the process of creating the perfect stuffie is so much fun." He leaned in conspiratorially. "Especially the adults. This town sure has a lot of Littles living in it, doesn't it?"

Rose nodded slowly, uncertain how he felt about that.

Deke winked at her. "Don't you worry. I'm a Daddy myself. I enjoy helping Littles choose their new stuffie."

Rose blew out a breath, relieved. It would sure be easier if she didn't have to keep lifestyle secrets from her new manager. Another strong point in favor of hiring Deke.

"See you tomorrow." He waved as he took off.

Rose was giddy as she went through the motions of closing up and getting the deposits ready. In no time at all, she was ready to go. As she headed through the nearly vacant mall toward the entrance where she had parked, she looked around for Johnny.

The man was nowhere to be found. By the time she reached the exit, she hadn't seen him. She glanced outside. She could see her car. It was in her line of sight. She'd left the mall alone dozens of times, but that had been before she'd met her Daddy.

Adam had been adamant about making sure she had someone with her when she headed to her car. He would be furious if he found out she'd taken a risk.

She really wanted to get home though. She wanted to be able to spend every moment of the rest of her evening with Daddy, not waste ten extra minutes waiting for him to come to the mall to help her walk a few yards. Even though she knew there was a spanking coming her way tonight, she still wanted to get home.

While she was hedging, she saw the usual group of teenagers come into view. They were milling around in the parking lot. They appeared to be laughing and shoving each other good-naturedly. She knew they looked up to her and wouldn't let anyone bother her.

Should she take the chance?

"You're being silly, Rose. Just go get in your car. It will be fine." She shoved through the doors and started walking briskly toward her car. An odd unease crept up her neck, but she tried to brush it off and walked faster.

Suddenly, she felt a presence behind her. Glancing over her shoulder, she saw two young men jogging toward her. They'd obviously been standing near the entrance, possibly against the wall. Waiting?

Rose had her satchel over her shoulder and across her body. She clutched it tightly and continued walking.

"Hey," someone shouted. She thought it came from the group of teenagers. "Leave her alone."

When she let her gaze shift in their direction, she found about six of them running toward her. A second later, someone grabbed the straps of her satchel and tugged so hard she lost her balance.

Rose screamed as loud as she could, hoping to get the attention of anyone else in the parking lot.

"Let her go," one of the teenagers yelled.

Suddenly, Rose was surrounded. The two men who were trying to get her bag had their hands on her, but the six teenagers were pulling them off.

Rose was scared out of her mind. Not just for herself but for the boys who'd come to her rescue.

The sound of screeching tires pierced the air, followed by a car door and then a deep voice she could never mistake.

Daddy.

She had no idea what he said because she was too scared to process words, but the men who'd attacked her released her and took off running. The teenagers parted for Adam to get to Rose, but they didn't give her much space.

A glance at their faces told her all of them were concerned.

"We got to her as fast as we could," the boy she'd seen talking to Adam the other night informed him. "Those thugs must have been waiting for her to come out."

Daddy grabbed Rose and hauled her into his arms, hugging her so tightly she could hardly breathe. When he finally let her go, he held her shoulders with both hands and looked down at her. "Are you okay, Rosebud?"

She nodded. She wasn't though. She was shaking. She was in shock. Scared out of her mind. Tears started to fall and then a flood of words. "I'm so sorry. I shouldn't have come out alone. I knew better. I thought it would be okay. I couldn't find Johnny and I didn't want to bother you and I saw the guys out here and assumed no one would try anything with them nearby and I just wanted to get home and..." She sobbed, sucking in breaths, close to hyperventilating.

"You're okay, Rose. Look at all the protectors you have gathered around you. Those bad guys didn't have a chance," Adam assured her.

With something else to focus on, Rose pulled herself back together. She slid from Adam's arms to hug every single teenager who had come to rescue her. "Thank you all so much —but don't do that again. They could have had a gun. I'm going to be much smarter from now on," she promised.

"That's a good thing, Stuff-It lady. What if we hadn't been here?" the spokesperson for the teenagers pointed out, making Rose smile faintly. *I bet he's a Daddy in the making?*

"I'm going to call the police to report the crime, guys. Would you all stay and talk to them as witnesses?" Adam asked.

"Sure, man. I think we know who they were. We won't snitch but we can point out where they ran to their cars so the cops can find them on the surveillance camera," the teenager suggested.

"I'm sure they'll appreciate any assistance you can give them," Adam assured them.

"What are your names?" Rose asked and noted them in her phone. "I want every single one of you to come make a stuffie on me."

When the boys tried to refuse, she insisted, "There has to be someone in your life who needs a squeezable friend. A little brother or sister? A girlfriend? Grandmother? You could even make one and donate it to a charity for a holiday present."

"My baby cousin would love one," a teenager shared.

"Come in this week and make one for them. All of you! Not everyone would have come to help me. You all did." She tried to keep the tears that suddenly welled back into her eyes from falling, but once they started, she couldn't stop.

"Rosebud," Adam whispered as he put his phone in his pocket. Tenderly, he wiped the tears from her face and hugged her close.

The teenagers elbowed each other as if trying to get someone to say the right thing. Quickly, their spokesman assured her, "We'll come in, Stuff-It lady."

"Rose. My name is Rose." She smiled through her tears as a police car pulled up next to the assembled group.

By the time the police finished their questions, it was late. Rose felt dead on her feet. Her day had been so filled with emotional turmoil. She didn't protest as Adam ushered her into his SUV. Her car would be fine in the parking lot overnight. She wasn't in any shape to drive anywhere.

Cuddling into the soft leather of the passenger seat, Rose felt her Daddy buckle her safely in place. She closed her eyes when he closed her door and blinked them open to make sure it was her Daddy who got in when the driver's door opened. Relieved, she relaxed again.

Without Rose having to mention a word, her Daddy drove straight to the bank. He even opened her satchel and made the deposit for her before taking off again.

When the car came to a stop the next time, she blearily allowed his guiding hands to coax her out of the car and into the warm house. Within a few minutes, Daddy had changed her into one of his T-shirts and she was curled up on a soft pillow in the large bed with her Daddy wrapped around her. Feeling cherished and protected, Rose tumbled into sleep.

Rose bolted upright as the shadowy figures tugged at the bag she had slung over her body. She had no idea what was inside but knew that she needed to protect it with her life. "No! Get away!" she shouted into the dark room.

When arms wrapped around her, she slapped at them, unwilling to let her assailant win. "No! You can't have it!"

"Rosebud, it's Daddy. You're okay, Little girl. You're safe," a deep voice reassured her as he pushed to sitting.

"No! You're not my Daddy!"

"Little girl! Open your eyes. I'm right here."

Cowering away, Rose peeked through her eyelashes to see Adam's handsome face inches away from her. The concern etched in his expression launched her forward into his arms. "Daddy! I was back there with those men."

"You're safe, Rosebud. I'm not going to let anyone harm you," he promised.

"I was so stupid. I stopped several times and knew I was making the wrong choice, but I kept going to my car," she whispered.

"Sometimes Little girls have to learn a lesson the hard way. I'm just glad that you're unharmed."

"I didn't listen to you. I should have listened."

When Adam didn't answer her, Rose leaned away to look at him. Swallowing hard, she said, "I think I need to be punished."

"Those bad guys are at fault, Rosebud," he reminded her gently.

"But I should have listened to you."

"Yes. From now on you take safety precautions even if you don't want to bother anyone or you think it's okay to walk the short distance to your car."

Rose nodded. She didn't know how Adam could always read her mind, but somehow he knew what she'd considered last night. "You're right."

She set a hand on his broad chest and felt his steady heartbeat against her palm. Leaning forward, Rose pressed a light kiss against his lips before rising to her knees on the mattress. She shifted to place herself face down over his lap.

"What do you need, Little girl?" His deep voice wrapped around her in the darkened room illuminated only by the nightlight in the attached master bathroom.

"I was bad."

"Do you need a spanking?"

Unable to tell him, she nodded her head, hoping he could see well enough to make her feel better.

"Daddy will help you, Rosebud. First, let's take off this T-shirt."

Strong hands tugged the soft material from under her tummy and pulled it over her head. He dropped it to the floor below where her head dangled over the side of the mattress. Cool air drifted over her nude body and Rose shivered. His hands stroked over her bare skin, warming her slightly.

"I want you to count to thirty, Little girl. Then your spanking will be finished and all your bad decisions from yesterday will be wiped away. Can you do that for Daddy?" he asked.

Thirty spanks exceeded the number of swats he'd given her in the past. She knew her bottom would burn after that many. Nodding her head again, she whispered, "Yes, Daddy."

"Good girl."

Without a warm-up, Adam dropped his hand to her bottom. The sting instantly made her body arch upward. Placing a restraining hand on the small of her back, he reminded her, "Count, Little girl."

"One," she whispered and froze as another landed as soon as she spoke. "Two."

Each one led to another until she wiggled on his lap. Her bottom burned with the heat of her punishment as Adam meted out the discipline she had earned and asked for. Tears dripped from her eyes to the floor.

When her punishment was almost halfway done, Rose reached back and wrapped her fingers around his wrist as her Daddy held her securely in place. She didn't try to tug it away but just needed to touch him. To her delight, he lifted his hand and intermeshed his fingers with hers before pressing both back into place to hold her safely on his lap.

"Thirteen, fourteen," she continued to count. The sting of each swat blurred together as that replay of the men attacking her disintegrated in her mind. She could think of nothing other than the feel of his hard thighs under her body and the impact of his hand on her bottom. Rose melted over his lap, ceding her control to this man.

"I love you, Daddy," she whispered between the numbers she recited.

"That's it, Little girl. You don't always have to do everything alone. Daddy loves you so much. I'm so proud of you."

"Twenty-seven. Twenty-eight."

When she finally could announce, "Thirty," her mind could only focus on his sweet encouragement and praise. She felt him lift her into his arms and cuddle her to his chest as he rocked her gently. Her Daddy stroked a hand over her hair and wiped the wetness of her tears from her cheeks.

"There's my sweet Baby. I think you need some time being a very Little girl for your Daddy. Let's get you a bottle," he comforted her gently.

She nodded against his chest. Her mouth dry after her tears and counting, she craved something to drink. She clung to him as he shifted to stand with her cradled in his arms. Her Daddy carried her to the nursery and placed her feet on the soft carpet. She stayed by his side as he quickly shook up a bottle of something from the minifridge under the changing table and swapped the flat lid for one that was nipple-shaped.

"Hold this for Daddy," he instructed. When she held it

securely, he scooped her back into his arms and carried her to the large, padded chair next to the crib.

"That's my good Little," he praised her as he took back the bottle and brushed the soft tip across her lips. "Drink, Rosebud."

Opening her mouth, she allowed him to insert the nipple and she sucked experimentally. A sweet, creamy mixture flowed into her mouth. It tasted so good. Rose cupped her hands over her Daddy's to hold the bottle close.

"Good, huh? I thought you'd like Daddy's special mixture."

She nodded and drank more. This bottle tasted even better than the one he'd given her the other night. There alone in the dark room with her Daddy, Rose allowed herself to drift into a very Little state of mind. Nothing mattered but being here with him as he took care of her. The fantasy that had lingered in her mind after reading about those Littles in books being cared for so intimately unfurled in her mind and she basked in his complete attention.

"Such a pretty Baby," he complimented her as he rocked her gently.

Rose closed her eyes as she sucked, exhaustion closing around her as she relaxed in his arms. Her Daddy wiggled the bottle when she nodded off and encouraged her to drink a little more. Snuggling closer, she continued to drink the delicious mixture. With her tummy full, Rose drifted on the edge of sleep.

"Let's get this pretty Baby ready for bed."

Adam lifted her back into his arms and carried her over to the padded top of the changing table. She shivered slightly at the feel of the cool surface under her. She wanted to be back in his embrace. Lifting her arms, Rose mumbled, "Daddy? Up."

"Soon, Rosebud. Daddy will hug you close." He moved away from her and returned quickly with her floppy-eared stuffie.

Kissing Ruff's soft fur, Rose hugged him close. He hadn't gone to work with her. Ruff would have protected her.

Her Daddy lifted her hips and placed something crinkly underneath her bottom. Moving efficiently, he wrapped it around her pelvis and attached it securely at the side. Adam leaned over her to kiss Rose softly.

"Now you're all ready to go to sleep. Daddy wants you close to him."

She nodded her agreement. Rose didn't want to be away from him. When he lifted her to her feet, she clung to his hand and walked unsteadily after him. The thick padding between her legs made her wobbly, but her Daddy supported her safely. When they reached the large bed, he placed her in the middle of the mattress before curling around her body.

Warm and protected, Rose crashed back into sleep.

Chapter Fifteen

"Mmm," Rose mumbled against her Daddy's chest. Blinking her eyes open, she looked into his handsome face. "Hi, Daddy," Rose greeted him with a smile.

"Hi, Baby girl. Did you sleep better after your bottle?"

She nodded and felt her face heat. Rose didn't know how she felt about being so Little. She brushed against the crinkly material wrapped around her hips. He'd dressed her in one of the diapers in the nursery. It scratched slightly against her, refreshing the sting of her punishment.

"I have to potty," she whispered.

"You could use your diaper," he suggested.

Without hesitating, she shook her head.

"You don't have to today."

She heard the implication in his tone that he would ask her to do this someday. Rose expected to feel embarrassed, but she felt comforted that he wanted to take care of her in all ways. When she nodded, he leaned forward to kiss her.

"Good girl. Let's go potty."

Adam walked her into the bathroom and removed her diaper. He waited nearby as she used the toilet. When she finished, he wiped her carefully and led her to the nursery.

"Daddy wants to make sure you feel well, Rosebud."

He boosted her onto the changing table and instructed, "On your hands and knees, Little girl. Leave your bottom in the air as you press your cheek to the padding. Thighs apart. That's my good girl."

Embarrassed by this position, Rose could only imagine what she looked like. She'd caught sight of herself in the large mirror as they'd passed. Her punished bottom was rosy red. In this position, she could feel her buttocks spread widely and knew he could see everything. Rose tried to shuffle her legs back together, but he held her solidly in position.

"No squirming, Little girl. You don't want to fall off the changing table."

She heard a squirt of something thick and turned to look but couldn't see anything. Freezing at the feel of his finger at her small, puckered opening, Rose whined, "Nooo!"

"Daddy's in charge, Little girl," he corrected her and pushed his finger deep into her tight passage to apply the slick lubricant thoroughly. "I'm going to take your temperature. Hold still."

Not wanting to acknowledge how this invasion turned her on, Rose tried to think of anything else when he slid his finger out and replaced it with a thick tube. Columns of numbers. New stuffies to order. A salary for Deke. Nothing distracted her from the feel of the cold thermometer her Daddy adjusted carefully in her bottom.

"Can it come out yet?" she begged, peeking back at him.

"Not yet, Rosebud. Soon," he promised, stroking her back before guiding his hand under her body. "Stay still."

He cupped one dangling breast and massaged it slightly before lightly pinching the nipple. At her quick inhale, he repeated the caress to the other side. "You are so pretty, Little girl. Perhaps you deserve a reward for doing exactly what Daddy tells you to do."

That tantalizing hand stroked over her tummy to trace her

lower lips. "Do you like Daddy taking care of you?" he asked. "You are so wet."

Rose hid her face in her hands and nodded. She couldn't lie to him.

"That's a good thing, Little girl. Let me check your temperature and I'll reward you for being so brave and telling me the truth. Stay in this position."

She felt him remove the tube and held her breath. What kind of reward did he have in mind?

"Your temperature is perfect, Little girl, but I think this bottom needs a reminder. I don't want you to forget the lesson you learned last night about trying to do too much by yourself."

"I'll remember!" she promised as she heard the door in the changing table open before something crinkly was removed. Rose wanted to look but she didn't. Squeezing her eyes shut, she pressed her face into her hands.

"Good girl."

Something cold and thick pressed against her bottom hole. Her eyes opened in shock as he pushed the device into her while she tried to push out the invader. Rose felt that tight ring of muscle she clenched so hard give to his insistence.

"Relax and let the plug settle in your bottom, Rosebud. It will help you remember everything Daddy wants you to do. Eat your lunch. Let others help you. Be safe when you leave the store."

"I can't wear this all day," she protested.

"You will. If you have to potty, take it out and put it back in. If you can't get it back in, call me. I'll run to the mall and fill this bottom immediately. Daddy will be able to tell if you don't wear it."

He adjusted it slightly and she moaned as shivers gathered inside her. She was so sensitive back there. The image of her Daddy taking her in this previously forbidden place jolted into her mind and she froze.

Adam patted her bottom reassuringly as he cleaned his hands with a handy wipe. "If I'm reading your body language correctly, you're wondering if I'll take you here."

He stroked between her legs and played in her wetness. Brushing his fingertips over her clit, Adam rewarded her bravery. When she moved restlessly on the changing table, rocking forward and back, he answered her question.

"Oh, yes, Little girl. I will be buried deep in this cute bottom. I'll take care to stretch your tight passage so you can take me with pleasure. This small reminder you wear today will be replaced with a bigger one and then another and so on until you're ready for me." A flick of his fingers against the small protective piece that lay outside jarred the device inside her.

"Perhaps someday, you'll beg me to fill you here."

The combination of the mental pictures he created in her mind combined with his touch pushed Rose into a massive climax. Her body contracted around the inserted plug as sensations burst over her. The pleasure was almost too much as he continued to stimulate her toward another orgasm.

When she was almost there, his fingers lifted from her. "What?" Rose protested, rising to her hands and knees to look around at him.

"No touching yourself until you get home tonight. Promise Daddy."

She looked at him in disbelief. She was so close. "I have to wait?"

"I'll be at the store before closing time to walk you out of the building. What is your reminder going to help you remember?" he asked, ignoring her struggle as he lifted her from the table and set her feet on the carpet.

When Rose didn't answer, he instructed, "Repeat after me. Eat lunch. Keep the reminder in your bottom. Call Daddy if you need help replacing the plug, and make sure you're protected as you leave the building."

Automatically, she repeated his directions.

"Good girl. Time to get dressed and go to work." He wrapped an arm around her waist and guided her back to the bedroom to dress, helping her move much more quickly than she would have on her own as the intruder inside her bottom shifted—a constant reminder of its presence.

Hours later, Rose flopped into her chair and froze as she pushed the device deeper. It wasn't keeping her from working. It just kept making its presence known. Opening her teddy bear lunchbox, Rose lifted out a napkin with a heart drawn on it by hand. Her Daddy's.

She liked being reminded that he loved her. After forcing herself to open the small container of grapes, she popped two into her mouth. When she turned over her napkin to wipe her hands, she discovered another message. *No touching!*

Sighing deeply, Rose opened her computer and checked her inventory. "I'm being good, Daddy." Her answer reverberated in the empty room.

"Oh, great. Now I'm talking to myself."

"You busy, boss?"

Rose looked up to see Deke's concerned face and knew her Daddy was right again. That reminder should keep her focused on her work, too.

"Don't mind me, Deke. This holiday rush is incredible. It will establish Stuff-It firmly in the community. I couldn't be more thrilled, but I need some help. If everything is under control out there, come take a seat. Let's talk."

For the next thirty minutes, the two sat and discussed goals and schedules. When they finished, Rose had a manager for her store. Deke headed out to make a late afternoon bank drop. They deemed that would be safer than leaving after dark from a deserted mall. Already it felt like a ton of weight had been lifted from her shoulders.

Between Deke taking on a lot of responsibilities and Larisa managing more of the marketing and social media, Rose felt like her team was complete. She could breathe easier.

Thanks, Daddy.

Chapter Sixteen

"Merry Christmas Eve, Little girl," Adam greeted Rose as he rushed to enter the Stuff-It store just as she closed the gate.

"I feel like we've done this before," she said with a laugh as she tugged him inside. It had been a busy few weeks, but Rose felt on top of the world. Things had really changed for her.

"It worked out pretty well for you to let me in the last time," he reminded her with a grin.

"It did," she agreed and pulled him a bit closer for a kiss before latching the door closed.

"Were you busy today?" he asked, looking around the store.

"You would never believe the tornado that came through here today. Deke implemented a new way to keep the place stocked and in order. He's so amazing. I think we'll be able to walk out the door at the end of the night without having so much to do after hours."

"I like the sound of that," he answered enthusiastically.

"I figured you would. Are you ready to go home?"

"I thought we might stop at a Christmas party tonight. Would you like to hang out with the other Littles at Blaze tonight?"

She looked at him and bounced on her exhausted toes. "I would love that. I'm sure they'll be a lot of fun."

"Let's go. Grab a Santa hat to wear and don't forget Ruff," he instructed.

"He'd be so upset to miss a party!"

In moments, they were headed down the road toward the adult club. She peeked over at him as butterflies gathered in her tummy. "I've never been to a place like Blaze."

"You'll like it. Everyone is very friendly. The Littles have their own area—the daycare. You don't have to go anywhere else, but I thought you might want to walk around with me to explore."

"Is it okay to watch other people..." her voice faded away and she whispered, "you know—do stuff?"

"There are private rooms if people wish to play without others seeing. Everyone else knows that others are watching. For some, that's part of the allure."

"Oh! Okay, then. I'd like to see what's going on," she admitted as he turned into the secluded parking lot.

Her Daddy escorted her through the front door where Tarson winked at her familiarly.

"You remember Tarson from Little Cakes, right?" Adam asked her as he shook the large man's hand. "He's Blaze's Dungeon Master. He makes sure everyone is safe as they explore things here at the club."

"Nice hat, Rose. Ellie and Daisy are coloring in the daycare if you want to join them," the Dungeon Master shared. "The Christmas party will be in the main room in a couple of hours."

"Daddy's going to show me around a bit before I join them. Is that okay?" she asked, holding Ruff against her tummy with hands that shook slightly.

"Of course. Your Daddy is a wise man. Littles are curious. It's better you explore with him so you can ask questions," Tarson assured her.

"Ready to go look around, Rosebud?" Adam asked.

"Yesss," she answered, nervously pulling out that last letter.

Adam took her hand and led her through the bar so she could wave to Riley. The tattooed bartender rushed from behind the bar to hug Rose. She was dressed like an elf in all green with a tool belt around her waist. Only the tools in the loops were bottles and shot glasses.

"Want a shot of eggnog? I have some with and without," Riley shared with Rose and Adam.

"I think we'll pass for now. Maybe at the party," Adam answered for them.

Rose nodded her agreement. She wanted to keep her head on straight as they explored. "We're going in there," she explained, waving at the door that separated the play area from the lounge.

"Your Daddy's going to show you around, huh? You'll love it. I'll see you in a while in the Little area. We'll answer any questions you have left over," Riley told her.

"Oh, Daddy said I could ask him anything," Rose assured her.

"That's good. But, if you have any left over or that you think of later," Riley rushed to add as she looked at Rose with wide eyes that jerked slightly toward Adam as Riley stared at Rose.

"Oh, yeah! That makes sense. If I think of anything later," Rose blurted as she finally caught on to Riley's underlying message that she could ask them anything she didn't want to ask her Daddy.

As they walked away, Rose quietly celebrated having friends who would give her the insider information. When her Daddy squeezed her hand, she realized he'd already said her name twice. "Yes, Daddy?"

"You can ask me anything, Rosebud." His gaze held hers until she nodded.

"Thanks, Daddy."

"Squeeze my hand if you want to stop and watch."

He walked slowly through the space. Each time she hesitated, Adam gripped her hand to remind her and paused. He would lean down to whisper information into her ear.

In one scene, a woman stretched over a spanking bench. She wore a schoolgirl uniform. The short plaid skirt was tossed over her back to bare her bottom. A stern-looking man spanked her with a large, ribbed paddle as she wailed.

Rose felt frozen in place. Somehow, she knew that woman. With a groan, the punished brat turned her face. Alice! There was no mistaking her even with the smeared mascara around her eyes. Slowly, Alice winked one eye before Adam led Rose away.

"That was Alice," Rose whispered, tipping her head back to look at Adam.

"Yes. Sometimes you'll see people you know at Blaze. Just remember to always respect their privacy and not mention it to them in front of other people."

Rose nodded agreement. "Yes, Daddy."

When they got to the aftercare area, Rose tugged him over to a chair.

"Do you want to sit in Daddy's lap?" he asked.

Rose nodded and clambered up onto his lap immediately. Rattled by all she had seen, Rose needed some time to process without any additional stimulation. Her Daddy didn't ask any questions but simply held her in his arms as he rocked her slowly.

Tarson walked by with a sippy cup and quietly set it on the small table next to the couple. Rose cuddled against her Daddy but heard Adam softly thank the large man.

"Here, Little girl. Drink some water. It will make you feel better," Adam suggested.

Gratefully, she took a sip and then several more. It was cool and crisp. Just what she needed.

"Rose, do you want to ask Daddy any questions? Are you concerned or upset by what you saw?"

She shook her head and then said, "No. That was what they

wanted to do. I realize everything is consensual. I might want to try a few things but not for a long while," she confessed.

"Are you glad I took you on a tour?"

"Yes. I would have worried about what was happening if you hadn't taken me around. Now I know and I can go have fun with my friends," she replied, pushing herself to sit up straight on his lap.

"Are you ready to go color?"

"Yes, please."

"What a polite Little girl," Adam complimented.

"This doesn't seem like a smart place to get in trouble," she admitted, remembering the intense spanking scene they'd passed.

Her Daddy's laugh made her giggle. Wow, did she have questions for the other Littles.

As soon as Adam left Rose alone with the other Littles, Riley rushed in and squeezed into the circle that had formed around the first-time visitor. Rose was in the middle of asking all sorts of questions when Tarson knocked on the top of one of the half-wall dividers around the daycare to get their attention.

His raised eyebrow told them he knew exactly what they were doing. Rose felt her cheeks flame with heat and knew she looked incredibly guilty. She tried to hide behind Daisy but his own Little didn't want to be directly in Tarson's view either. Their scrambling behind one another became a game that all the Littles were drawn into, and giggles filled the area.

"Littles?" Tarson's deep voice made them all freeze and turn to look at him.

"I would like to introduce you to a new Little who would like to play with you. Everyone, say 'Hi!' to Kiki."

"Hi, Kiki!" everyone parroted back almost in unison.

"Play nice, Littles," Tarson advised before he disappeared to retake his position at the door.

"So, who's a brat here?" Kiki asked brazenly.

"Mmm, probably none of us," Tori answered quietly, before leaning forward to ask conspiratorially, "Are you?"

"Totally!" Kiki confirmed with a big grin.

"Don't you get spanked a lot?" Daisy asked.

"I would if I had a Daddy, but I don't so I do what I want," Kiki answered before looking around at their faces. "Fuck! You all have Daddies, don't you? Are there any more around?"

"Of course. My Daddy says there are a lot of Daddies looking for their Littles," Riley answered.

The jingle of loud sleigh bells preceded a booming announcement, "Ho, ho, ho! Bring your holiday cheer and gather in the lounge for the Christmas Eve party."

Ellie rushed to the half wall to pick up a tote bag of goodies. Suddenly she turned toward the rest of the Littles, her eyes wide. "Hey, look, Tori! Your brother's here to celebrate as well!" Ellie pointed toward the handsome new arrival.

"Hi, Terry!" Tori called and waved furiously. All the Littles joined in, even the newest arrival.

Terry stopped by briefly to greet everyone. Rose noticed that his eyes paused on the newcomer, and Kiki snuck glances his way as well. Rose wondered if Tori's brother was a Daddy. She decided to ask that question as soon as he left.

"Terry!" a female voice called.

At the sound of another woman approaching, Rose noticed Kiki's straight posture wilt a bit.

"Sorry, Little girls. I better find out what that's all about. Come join the party," Terry suggested before leaving.

"He's a Daddy," Kiki announced with certainty.

"He is a Daddy," Tori confirmed. "How could you tell?"

"It was written all over him," Kiki answered.

"Before you go, I've got a small gift for you." Ellie rushed to give everyone a small cupcake box holding the special flavor for the holiday.

"Ooo! A Santa's Kiss cupcake. And what's this? A coloring book?" Rose exclaimed before rushing forward to hug Ellie.

"Thank you so much. I'm sorry I don't have anything for you. I didn't know we were exchanging gifts."

"You've already given me your present. I love seeing you every time you come in to try a cupcake."

Rose turned to watch everyone reveal their own favorite flavors: Rainbow Sprinkles, Lemon Chiffon, Blue Raspberry, Red Velvet, Pink Lemonade, Black Forest, Witch's Brew, Pumpkin Spice, and Santa's Kiss. Ellie had even brought one extra one in case someone new joined them.

Kiki opened the box and lifted it to her nose. "Holy shit! This smells so chocolatey. What's it called?"

"Fudge Crunch," Ellie said with a smile. "You're going to love it."

"I know I will. Thank you," Kiki said with a genuine smile as she carefully replaced the lid to preserve the cupcake.

"Rosebud? Are you coming?" Adam leaned on the barrier protecting the Little space.

His expression was tender. She loved that he smiled at everyone but had a special look for her alone. There was no doubt in her mind that her Daddy loved her. It made her all warm and fluttery inside.

Rose nodded quickly. "On my way, Daddy. Ruff and I wouldn't miss this for anything."

Author's Note

We hope you're enjoying Little Cakes! We are so excited to be working together to create this new series! More stories will be coming soon!

Little Cakes:
(by Pepper North and Paige Michaels)
Rainbow Sprinkles
Lemon Chiffon
Blue Raspberry
Red Velvet
Pink Lemonade
Black Forest
Witch's Brew
Pumpkin Spice
Santa's Kiss
Fudge Crunch
Sweet Tooth
Flirty Kumquat
Birthday Cake
Caramel Drizzle

Maraschino Cherry
Reindeer Tracks

About Pepper North

Ever just gone for it? That's what *USA Today* Bestselling Author Pepper North did in 2017 when she posted a book for sale on Amazon without telling anyone. Thanks to her amazing fans, the support of the writing community, Mr. North, and a killer schedule, she has now written more than 70 books!

Enjoy contemporary, paranormal, dark, and erotic romances that are both sweet and steamy? Pepper will convert you into one of her loyal readers. What's coming in the future? A Daddypalooza!

Connect with me on your favorite platform!
I'm also having fun on TikTok as well!

amazon.com/author/pepper_north

bookbub.com/profile/pepper-north

facebook.com/AuthorPepperNorth

instagram.com/4peppernorth

pinterest.com/4peppernorth

twitter.com/@4peppernorth

Pepper North Series

Dr. Richards' Littles®

A beloved age play series that features Littles who find their forever Daddies and Mommies. Dr. Richards guides and supports their efforts to keep their Littles happy and healthy.

Available on Amazon

SANCTUM

Pepper North introduces you to an age play community that is isolated from the surrounding world. Here Littles can be Little, and Daddies can care for their Littles and keep them protected from the outside world.

Available on Amazon

Soldier Daddies

What private mission are these elite soldiers undertaking? They're all searching for their perfect Little girl.

Available on Amazon

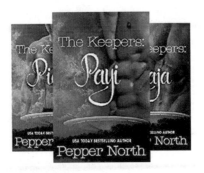

The Keepers

This series from Pepper North is a twist on contemporary age play romances. Here are the stories of humans cared for by specially selected Keepers of an alien race. These are science fiction novels that age play readers will love!

Available on Amazon

The Magic of Twelve

The Magic of Twelve features the stories of twelve women transported on their 22nd birthday to a new life as the droblin (cherished Little one) of a Sorcerer of Bairn. These magic wielders have waited a long time to take complete care of their droblin's needs. They will protect their precious one to their last drop of magic from a growing menace. Each novel is a complete story.

Available on Amazon

About Paige Michaels

Paige Michaels is a USA Today bestselling author of naughty romance books that are meant to make you squirm. She loves a happily ever after and spends the bulk of every day either reading erotic romance or writing it.

Other books by Paige Michaels:

The Nurturing Center:
Susie
Emmy
Jenny
Lily
Annie
Mindy

Eleadian Mates:
His Little Emerald
His Little Diamond
His Little Garnet
His Little Amethyst
His Little Sapphire
His Little Topaz

Littleworld:
Anabel's Daddy
Melody's Daddy

Haley's Daddy
Willow's Daddy
Juliana's Daddy
Tiffany's Daddy
Felicity's Daddy
Emma's Daddy
Lizzy's Daddy
Claire's Daddy
Kylie's Daddy
Ruby's Daddy
Briana's Daddies
Jake's Mommy and Daddy
Luna's Daddy
Petra's Daddy
Littleworld Box Set One
Littleworld Box Set Two
Littleworld Box Set Three
Littleworld Box Set Four

Holidays at Rawhide Ranch:
Felicity's Little Father's Day
A Cheerful Little Coloring Day

If you'd like to see a map of Regression island where Littleworld
is located, please visit my website: PaigeMichaels.com

facebook.com/PaigeMichaelsAuthor

amazon.com/author/PaigeMichaels

bookbub.com/authors/paige-michaels

Afterword

If you've enjoyed this story, it will make our day if you could leave an honest review on Amazon. Reviews help other people find our books and help us continue creating more Little adventures. Our thanks in advance. We always love to hear from our readers what they enjoy and dislike when reading an alternate love story featuring age-play.

Made in the USA
Columbia, SC
25 September 2024

42964835R10100